CYBER RONIN

The Phantom Firewall

SCOTT BARNES

CYBER ZEN PUBLISHING

This Book Was Brought to You By...

One Cybersecurity Nerd + One AI That Doesn't Sleep. Let's clear the air: Did I use ChatGPT to help write this book? *Absolutely.* Did it write it *for* me while I sat on a beach sipping coffee? *Not unless that beach had a SIEM dashboard and a SOC on fire.*

Here's the truth: I've spent decades navigating cybersecurity landmines, building defenses, and untangling digital messes. This book came from *that*. The characters, decisions, and storylines were built from real-world lessons (some learned the hard way).

But writing a "decide your destiny" cybersecurity adventure book? That's a lot of plotting, editing, and naming chapters something better than *Chapter 87: Uh Oh.* So yes—AI helped me brainstorm, polish sentences, and occasionally say, *"Maybe don't use the word 'cyber-doom' three times in one paragraph."*

In short: I brought the ideas. The AI helped carry the groceries. This book is the result of both—*human creativity with machine assistance.* So, if you're reading this and *wondering, "Was this written by ChatGPT?"* Rest assured: Only the boring parts. And I deleted those.

— *S.B.*

How to Play

Welcome to *Cyber Ronin: The Phantom Firewall* — a **Decide Your Destiny** cybersecurity adventure.

You're stepping into a high-stakes corporate cyber crisis, where every decision shapes your fate.

At the end of each chapter, you'll be presented with options and directed to a numbered path: [**Chapter #**]

Make your choice. Turn to the chapter. Live (or die) with the consequences.

Some paths lead to success. Others end in failure. Many reveal truths you weren't meant to find.

- **Unlock hidden badges**
- **Collect Ronin Wisdom**
- **Survive the digital shadows**

Good luck!

Chapter 1

Smell of Burnt Silicon

The elevator jerks slightly before groaning open on the 12th floor, where Kensei Systems' cybersecurity team resides—or what's left of it.

The air hits you first: bitter coffee clinging to the warm tang of ozone—like an old server room pushing its luck for too long.

Overhead lights flicker with the confidence of a CISO during a congressional hearing. The entire floor hums—machines working harder than people. You're not sure if that's a metaphor yet.

You step out. No one greets you. No welcome banner. Just a flickering whiteboard, half-erased incident response steps still visible. A sticky note, slightly curled at the edges, reads:

"Trust nothing. Logs lie. - R."

Your name badge isn't activated, so you push open the SOC door with your shoulder and find what can only be described as a scene from a Netflix breach documentary:

- One analyst asleep in a hoodie beneath a blinking **"All Clear"** alert.

- Monitors frozen mid–KQL query.

- A Slack notification blinking persistently in the corner of a dusty screen.

You settle into the desk that was presumably yours. The chair still holds the imprint of the last person who sat there. You wonder what they knew—and how fast they left.

You weren't supposed to be here.

Not yet.

You were brought in on short notice—contractor, consultant, temp.

The last CISO left mid–incident and no one's filled in the blanks. Legal handed you admin access before HR even printed your badge.

Your inbox is a digital crime scene: broken handoffs, locked–out analysts, audit trails that don't line up.

The only orientation you got? Three folders labeled:

Transition, Legacy Risks, and Do Not Touch.

*"It wasn't much of an orientation packet — just a badge that didn't scan, a stack of generic HR papers, and three folders clipped together with **The Packet** scrawled across the cover."*

You opened all of them.

Booting up your system, the login screen briefly glitches before re-solving itself. You frown. Probably nothing. But your gut doesn't believe in coincidence. Not anymore.

The Slack window finally loads, and the first message comes in—without a sound.

Slack Message - TestAcct–1129

They're already in.

You have 72 hours before they trigger the detonation protocol.

If you want to live—and keep your reputation—

start with the firewall. It's not what it seems.

Before you can respond, the message auto–deletes.

You freeze. Then you investigate that account... shouldn't exist.

Not anymore. A test user account marked decommissioned three years ago. Disabled. Archived. Gone.

Except it just spoke to you.

Your heartbeat taps a new rhythm in your chest. Is this a test? A prank? A remnant script misfiring in the system?

No.

This is the work of someone who knows the inside of this network better than you. Better than anyone. And they've chosen you.

You glance around the room—still silent, still humming. The only sound is the faint rattle of a ceiling vent and the growing storm of possibilities swirling in your mind.

This isn't **onboarding.**

It's initiation.

You crack your knuckles and breathe once, slowly, through your nose.

Let the breach begin.

What do you do first?

[2] Trace the Test Account Activity

Someone just resurrected a ghost. You're going to find out where it walked—and why.

[3] Scan the Firewall Configurations

If the message is right, the firewalls not just misconfigured—it's compromised.

[4] Notify Executive Leadership

Panic early or explain later? Maybe someone at the top already knows.

[5] Walk Away

You weren't hired for this. Close the laptop. Pretend you didn't see the message.

Chapter 2

Trace the Test Account Activity

The screen glows like a heartbeat as you open the SIEM dashboard. **TestAcct-1129** stares back at you—mocking everything you thought you knew about **"decommissioned"** credentials.

You pull audit logs. It's been active. Not once. Not occasionally. But **regularly**—every few days, always between 2:00 and 2:15 a.m., when most of the network is quiet and no change windows are scheduled.

No one noticed. Or maybe someone did—and chose not to say anything.

You narrow the timeline and filter by source IP.

There it is.

Login Time: 02:07:16

Source IP: 10.4.99.25

CMDB Lookup: No Match Found

You frown.

You run the same query across firewall logs.

Connection detected: TestAcct-1129 ⊠ \\DC–LEGACY01.internal.kensei.local

Command executed: firewall_export.ps1

Duration: 14 seconds

Privileges: Admin

Your pulse spikes.

This wasn't **recon.**

They knew exactly where to go.

And they had **admin privileges.**

You freeze.

DC–LEGACY01

That name rings a bell—buried in the audit file chaos from Day One. One of those systems flagged as "transition in progress" or "decommissioned." At the time, it seemed like just another forgotten relic.

But now it's here. Live.

And someone's logging into it with credentials that should've been ash. Something's off.

No one should be able to access that system without tripping at least one alert—unless they knew how to disable those alerts first.

You expand your query. You find additional anomalies:

• **Folder accessed:** \\SHARE\M&A\Transition\ShadowLegal

• **Script executed:** silent_exfil.sh

• **Outbound connection:** Encrypted tunnel (flagged as "internal testing")

You've seen this pattern before.

But only in red team exercises.

This... this is precision work.

Suddenly, a memory stirs. The sticky note.

"Trust nothing. Logs lie. R."

You sit back for a moment, reading the data again—not just looking for anomalies but for misdirection.

Whoever used this account didn't just want data. They wanted plausible deniability. They built in noise. Left behind false flags. And they knew just enough to make this look like a test script run by an old SOC engineer.

Your coffee's gone cold.

The office is still **asleep.**

You're not.

What do you do next?

[6] Remote into DC–LEGACY01

You want to see what they saw—and what they left behind.

[7] Physically Inspect the Server Room

There are ghosts in that hardware. You need to see it with your own eyes.

[8] Run a Containment Playbook

You don't have time to dig—just eliminate the threat before it spreads.

[9] Ping Your Old Homeland Threat Response Contact

If this is what you think it is, you're going to need off-the-books help.

Chapter 3

Scan the Firewall Configurations

Start with the firewall. It's not what it seems.

The message echoes as you load the console.

Normally, you'd scoff—paranoia loves perimeter gear.

But something about the silence in this building, the rogue credentials, and that long-forgotten server puts you on edge.

There's something deeply unsettling about the firewall interface.

Not the alerts. Not the architecture.

Just... the silence.

The dashboard loads without error, like a guilty man who smiles too much during questioning.

You know better.

Most firewalls smell. Figuratively.

You know the kind—duct-taped together by interns with Google certs and vibes.

But this one? It's worse.

It's quiet. Overly quiet.

You crack your knuckles, bring up the rule set, and scroll through the configuration.

At first glance, it looks fine. Ports, protocols, mappings... nothing jumps out.

Then you notice it: **Rule 78**.

Rule 78

• No name

- No description

- Source: Local Trusted Admin Override

- Destination IP: Unregistered

- Modified: 04:04 a.m. — April 1st

- Signature: Ronin-Bypass-Protocol

- Modified by: R. System

You lean in.

"Ronin-Bypass-Protocol"

The sticky note flashes in your mind:

"TRUST NOTHING. LOGS LIE. R."

So it was real. Not paranoia. Not corporate folklore whispered between SOC analysts at 2 a.m.

You try to disable the rule.

The console freezes.

Then restarts.

A message appears:

"Nice try. You're not ready."

No button. No logs. Just those five words before it drops you back to the top of the page like nothing happened.

You blink. Once. Twice.

You try again—navigating around the GUI into the CLI.

You run a config hash check—

but the checksums don't match.

Something's intercepting your request. Spoofing the response. Lying in the logs.

Your console freezes—just for a second.

Then the screen snaps back, like nothing happened.

But something's different.

A USB drive is plugged into the front of your tower.

Definitely not yours.

You didn't insert it. And no one else should've had access to this machine.

The label, scrawled in faded Sharpie:

Blade Protocol // Phase 1

Your screen dims.

An EDR alert flashes in the corner:

Possible Rogue USB Detected

Recommendation: Disconnect or Investigate Immediately

Your hand hovers.

You don't plug in mystery drives on instinct—at least, not without gloves and regret.

This wasn't a leftover.

It was planted. For you.

What do you do next?

[10] Plug the USB into a Sandbox Environment

The label looks deliberate. This might be your only clue.

[11] Isolate the Firewall from the Network

Whatever's behind this rule might already be exfiltrating.

[12] Ping a Red Team Contact for Help

You need someone paranoid—and off the books.

[13] Keep Digging into Logs

Not your first. Probably not your last.

Chapter 4

Notify Executive Leadership

You're not even sure you're ready.

Interim roles are supposed to come with less fire and more documentation.

You stare at the screen, blinking past the words:

"Nice try. You're not ready."

Well, you weren't ready either—not for a firewall that talks back, not for a resurrected test account with admin-level ghost access, and definitely not for a USB drive labeled **"Blade Protocol//Phase 1"** — plugged in like some **digital Excalibur.**

You take a breath. One hand on the desk, the other already reaching for the secure comms channel.

Your gut says act. Your experience says document. But your career? It says don't make enemies too early.

Still, your internal compass—that battered relic forged from years of red team drills, post-breach caffeine shakes, and boardroom damage control—won't let this sit.

You hesitate, fingers paused above the keyboard.

You don't want to be *that person* on Day Two, yelling **"breach"** like it's your full-time job.

But your gut—and the logs—aren't bluffing.

You open a blank message.

Subject: [URGENT] Suspicious Activity - Firewall Behavior & Legacy Credential Access

Tone: *Direct. Factual. No alarms. Just enough to provoke action—without triggering legal's ulcer.*

Summary:

– Reactivated test account accessing legacy domain controller

– Firewall rule with no audit trail, responding to encrypted outbound traffic

– Admin interface showing tampered behavior, potential manipulation

– Indicators suggest insider knowledge or prepositioned access

Risk:

– Potential insider breach

– Active persistence mechanisms

– Silent exfiltration in progress

Recommendation:

– Isolate affected systems immediately

– Initiate internal war–room engagement

Signed:

Incident Response Lead, Temp Assignment

(*Still technically onboarding*)

You read it twice. Then again.

No typos. No overreach. Just enough to raise red flags without setting the whole company on fire.

You hit send.

Then wait.

Five minutes.

Ten.

Twelve minutes later, a **Slack ping arrives from the CIO**. Short and brutal:

> *"Appreciate the heads up. We're in final Board prep—*
>
> ***don't escalate**. Review Friday."*

Friday?

You reread it. Twice.

The firewall just taunted you.

The logs are rotting.

And you're told to schedule around PowerPoint decks?

Your stomach tightens. Not from fear—from clarity.

They're not ignoring it.

They're compartmentalizing it.

And that's worse.

You glance at the blinking cursor on your screen.

There's no button to push. No AI to summon. Just you.

The Phantom isn't your only adversary.

Turns out, bureaucracy spreads faster than malware—and deletes the truth just as quietly.

What do you do next?

[14] Ignore Orders and Declare an Internal Security Event

Better to be wrong and hated than right and too late.

[15] Leak Sanitized Details to a Reporter

Force executive action from the outside. You didn't start this—but maybe you can end it.

[16] Call a Secret All-Hands with the SOC Team

If the leadership won't act, your team will.

[17] Go Rogue and Activate the Cyber Ronin Protocol

There are legends of a hidden defense program buried in the stack. Maybe this is why you were brought in.

Chapter 5

Walk Away

"Sometimes the hardest decision isn't what to fight—

It's whether to fight at all."

You sit back, the chair creaking beneath the weight of a choice that feels too heavy for your second day.

Your fingers hover over the keyboard, but they don't move.

You look around the office.

There's no one else here. Not really. Just bodies in chairs, Slack avatars glowing green out of obligation. Everyone's heads are down, drowning in alerts they stopped questioning weeks ago.

The Slack message is gone.

The logs? Inconclusive.

The firewall? Still humming its innocent lie.

No alarms. No war room. No one screaming.

But deep down, something screams anyway.

It lingers—like a loaded weapon with no fingerprints.

Maybe this isn't your problem.

You tell yourself you weren't equipped.

No briefings. No real access. Just firehose-level exposure and a half-burned inbox.

You tell yourself, *if they really cared,* they would've empowered you.

But you know the truth.

You saw enough to act.

And chose not to.

You didn't come here to fight ghost accounts and silent rules.

You came here to advise. Strategize. **Consult.**

You close the lid of your laptop slowly, deliberately.

A soft click echoes as it shuts—final, like a judgment handed down.

You stand. No one notices.

The SOC's big wall display still blinks **"All Clear"** in soft green lettering—as if belief alone could make it true. You take one last look.

There's an alert in the corner—barely visible. Something about encrypted outbound traffic from a legacy system.

It's labeled as **"False Positive // M&A Testing // Do Not Escalate"**

You don't open it.

You take the elevator down, past the buzzing lights, past the server room hum, past the receptionist who doesn't look up.

The city air hits you with static as you step outside.

The sky is gray. So is your gut.

Three days later, the breach hits the newswire like a data-driven grenade.

"Shadow credentials compromise 30M records.

Merger halts indefinitely."

"Kensei Systems rocked by insider ghost exploit."

No mention of you.

No quotes. No email trails.

Just silence.

The kind you earned.

Your phone buzzes. A recruiter.

"Exciting. Low stress. Great culture."

You swipe it away.

GAME OVER: *The Path of Silence*

You walked away. The breach didn't. Now the silence belongs to you.

Badge Earned: *"The Consultant Who Knew Too Little"*

Cyber Ronin Wisdom: *"He who walks away may live to consult another day—but someone else pays the price."*

Chapter 6

Remote into DC-LEGACY01

You click without thinking—instinct overriding protocol.

The connection initiates.

No MFA. No endpoint challenge.

Just a clean, silent handshake.

That's not normal.

That's surgical.

You're in.

DC–LEGACY01 loads to your screen—alive and operational.

No listing in the asset inventory. No DNS entry.

It shouldn't exist.

And yet... here it is. Humming. Waiting.

First Red Flag.

The desktop loads. **Windows Server 2008 R2.**

Wallpaper: default.

Start menu: disabled.

Taskbar: empty—except for a small green terminal blinking in the corner.

You don't click it. Not yet.

First, you launch your forensic capture tool.

You learned that lesson the hard way on a consulting gig in Dubai:

if it looks haunted, hit record.

You scan the running processes.

One stands out:

KAGEMUSHA.EXE

Running since: 03:14:07

Parent process: SYSTEM

You pause.

You've heard the term before—in a red team talk, whispered over whiskey: a **kagemusha** was a body double, a decoy sent to die in place of the real leader.

A shadow warrior.

A trap.

Your throat tightens.

This box isn't just alive—it's been staged.

Someone's using it as bait.

But for who?

You finally maximize the terminal window.

PROJECT KAGEMUSHA: Initiate or Observe?

The cursor blinks. Slowly. Tauntingly.

You glance at your packet capture.

Traffic is light—internal only. Pings. Failed auth attempts.

Nothing outbound.

Then something else catches your eye.

Scheduled Task: REBUILD_PPTX

Runs nightly at 2:17 a.m.—same time as the account activity.

You trace its output:

\\SHARE\M&A\Transition\ShadowLegal\BoardReady\

You scroll through the files.

Not logs.

Slides.

Narratives.

Curated screenshots.

Sanitized timelines.

This isn't about containment.

It's about spin control.

Someone isn't just hiding the breach—they're rehearsing it.

You return to the terminal.

INITIATE or OBSERVE?

The terminal blinks.

You hesitate.

Then—before you can decide—**a flicker.**

The screen splits.

Another session connects. From your IP.

But you're already here.

No prompt. No alert.

Just a second user, gliding through the interface like they've done this a hundred times.

They're not exploring.

They're **extracting.**

One command:

powershell

robocopy \\DC–LEGACY01\ShadowLegal

C:\temp\2023_docs /MIR /ZB /LOG+:stealth.txt

They copy everything—quietly, precisely, like it's scripted.

The session name?

user: R.OPS.ARCH

Then—just as quickly—it ends.

The user vanishes.

The terminal resets.

The logs wipe.

You're left staring at a blinking cursor.

No prompt.

No clue.

Just the cold certainty:

you weren't the one doing the watching.

What do you do next?

[18] Type Observe — Watch, Learn, Gather More Intel

If this is a decoy, maybe it's showing you what it wants you to see. Maybe that's the key.

[19] Type INITIATE — Trigger the Hidden Protocol

You've already touched the tripwire. Might as well see what goes off.

[20] Disconnect and Wipe All Traces — Clean Exit

This is deeper than you're ready for. No shame in regrouping.

[21] Screenshot Protocol

You'll need allies. Or a dead man's switch.

Chapter 7

Physically Inspect the Server Room

The elevator descends like corporate decision-making: slow, creaky, and filled with the promise of disappointment.

Sub-basement B2. The lights dim. The walls sweat. The air smells like dust, ozone, and secrets.

You badge in. A faint buzz. A red flash.

ACCESS DENIED.

Of course.

You glance around—then slide a fingernail under the loose corner of the card reader.

There's a manual release latch.

Because of course there is.

One click. One push. You're in.

The server room is not what you expected.

It's not the Hollywood neon of cool blue LEDs and sterile cables.

Its entropy made physical—rows of neglected servers, discarded chairs, and ancient Dell towers running systems that no one claims ownership of anymore.

Your boots crunch on a forgotten piece of plastic. A broken USB stick, probably. You step over a coil of Cat5e that's seen more service than half the team upstairs.

At the far end, under a flickering motion sensor light, is **DC-LEGACY01.**

It hums, not with power—but with purpose.

It's older than it should be, beige where everything else is black, and humming with that faint pitch only hardware of a certain vintage makes—the whine of spinning disks that still believe they're important.

A sticky note on its front panel reads:

"DO NOT TOUCH – Transition Testing –

Signed: OPS–R"

You kneel. Plug in your portable display.

The monitor comes to life.

No desktop. Just a terminal window.

The same one you saw remotely.

It flashes:

"PROJECT KAGEMUSHA"

A heartbeat later:

"Observer Mode: Live Feed Active"

You check the NIC lights.

Blinking. Too much traffic for idle.

This system isn't sleeping. **It's broadcasting.**

You trace the ethernet cable... and find it snaking into a side panel rigged behind what looks like HVAC access.

This isn't just rogue IT.

This is **intentional shadow infrastructure.**

Something shifts—the lights buzz faintly. A shadow blinks across the far rack.

Then you hear it:

Footsteps.

Deliberate. Heavy.

Someone else is in the server room.

You back into the shadows, duck behind a column of retired firewall appliances stacked like forgotten sentinels.

The door creaks. A figure steps in.

Black hoodie. Ballcap. Sleek black case in hand.

They move with confidence, not curiosity.

They approach DC–LEGACY01 and kneel just as you did.

They connect a device—a portable drive, maybe encrypted, maybe not—and begin typing commands you can't see.

You hold your breath.

Then you hear it—spoken quietly, like a farewell:

"Goodnight, Ronin. Time to vanish."

Like a stage actor taking their final bow.

The figure slides the side panel of the server open and slips something inside.

Then they stand, unplug the device, and walk toward the exit.

As the door swings shut, they pause.

And glance back.

You duck behind the rack, heart pounding.

Did they see you?

You wait.

Fifteen seconds. Thirty. **Nothing.**

When you emerge, the system is shut down.

The drive is gone.

The terminal window? **Closed.**

But the fan still spins—soft, steady, like it's trying to forget what it just saw.

And on the floor, half-tucked beneath the rack, is a folded slip of paper. You unfold it.

The paper smells of ozone and ink—and the handwriting is unmistakable.

Next time, knock. —R.

What do you do next?

[22] Pull the Plug and Run

Whatever this is, it's above your clearance—and your pay grade.

[23] Hide and Observe Who Enters Next

If someone else shows up, maybe you're not the only ghost chasing shadows.

[24] Confront Them With Your Phone Recording

Expose the operation in real time—if you're ready to make enemies.

[25] Trigger the Fire Suppression System

When in doubt: smoke, mirrors, and CO_2 can buy time.

Chapter 8

Run a Containment Playbook

You've seen enough.

Legacy accounts logging into shadow servers.

Executives downplaying anomalies.

Firewall rules with no fingerprints.

You don't need another meeting.

You need containment.

You pull up your secured admin console, already scripting. It's like walking into a digital warehouse with a flamethrower and yelling **"pest control."**

You filter Active Directory for all non-human accounts:

- Last login older than 90 days

- Assigned to systems no longer listed in asset inventory

- Holding privileged roles without justification

Result: *217 accounts matched*

Examples:

- svc_sftp_bob2007

- test_jane01_legacy

- admin_temp_migration

- keep_this_active_DO_NOT_DISABLE

That one gets flagged twice.

You expand your scope.

Add in orphaned service principals from cloud integrations.

Add in accounts created by… no one?

You blink. One SID resolves to a **deleted admin account** but is still assigned as an owner on five production containers.

You shake your head and add it to the purge list.

Command:

.\Purge-LegacyAccounts.ps1 –Scope All –Mode DryRun

You test first. Always test. You're not a barbarian.

The simulation reveals impact to:

- Sales reporting platform

- Marketing's image pipeline

- Internal dashboard used by the CFO

- "BirthdayBot," the Slack tool for birthday alerts

Not exactly critical infrastructure—but neither is the CFO's dashboard.

And if you kill the wrong thing, **someone important will notice.**

You smirk. **BirthdayBot goes down with the ship.**

The real kicker? The Dev team's entire test cluster—still tied to svc_intern_deploy.

No documentation. No warning.

You pause.

The risk is high—but so is doing nothing. Every minute these accounts exist, your attack surface remains wide open.

You toggle from dry run to **live**.

Command:

Invoke-AccountPurge –Scope Legacy –Mode Execute –NotifySe-curity

You hit **enter**.

And then... the screams begin.

You sit back—not smug, not sorry.

Just steady.

This isn't sabotage.

It's survival.

First come the emails.

Then the Slack messages.

Then—footsteps. Two people sprinting through the hallway toward IT like their code is on fire.

"WHO KILLED SALESFORCE ACCESS??"

"Why is our dashboard GONE?!"

"Did someone just delete my staging environment?

I swear..."

You take a breath.

And exhale.

This is what progress sounds like.

You don't gloat.

You document.

Timestamps. Account names. Privileges. Justifications. Everything by the book—or at least, the version of the book you're writing in real time.

Then you open a new Slack channel: #legacy-lockdown

You pin a message at the top:

Welcome to Day Zero of a Secure Environment.

Half the company is furious.

But the other half?

They're watching.

And somewhere beneath the chaos, you feel it—**the tide is shifting.**

What do you do next?

[26] Explain Calmly and Hold Your Ground

Sometimes, leading means being unpopular for the right reasons.

[27] Blame an Automation Bug (Sort of True…)

You can always restore a little credibility with plausible denial.

[28] Undo Everything and Re-Risk the Environment

Better to retreat than be crucified. Right?

[29] Call a Team War Room and Start Building Champions

You've started the fire. Now build the fire brigade.

Chapter 9

Ping Your Old Homeland Threat Response Contact

You close the chat window, lean back in your chair, and stare at the fire you just lit across half the company.

Marketing's **angry**.

Sales is **panicking**.

DevOps is drafting a **hit list**.

You? You feel it: **the shift**.

Not in permissions. In posture.

But what you don't have is time.

You open a secure messaging app—one that was never officially approved, but rides under the radar like a digital ninja.

You scroll through aliases.

Past ghosts. Burned ops. Disavowed agents.

Then—there it is: **DeadClock**.

A myth in Homeland Threat Response.

A ghost with clearance levels no one could trace.

You met once—briefly—during a red team exercise that went off-script and off-the-books.

You send a message:

> ***"Need eyes on a ghost firewall, dead account resurrection, and a project called KAGEMUSHA. You still in?"***

A pause.

Then the reply:

> ***"You found the Blade Protocol?"***

"Stay offline. Disable telemetry. This goes beyond corporate."

"Sending you a key."

The message evaporates in real time.

Ten seconds later, your secondary laptop pings.

No sender. No fanfare.

Just an encrypted archive labeled with a fingerprint hash and a single word:

PROVE

You run your private key through the decryption script.

Inside:

• **RONINEDGE**

A zero-day scanner you've never seen before

• **ObsidianSniff**

A packet sniffer tuned to ignore decoys and span port noise

• **rogue_hosts.yaml**

Rogue IPs linked to known APT groups—active during mergers and executive transitions

And one final note:

"The Phantom Firewall isn't config. It's behavioral.

It learns you."

"If it knows you're watching… it starts watching back."

—D

You stare at your screen.

This isn't a misconfiguration.

It's a system with intent.

A perimeter that hides its hunger behind clean dashboards and policy lies.

You glance at your own telemetry.

Outbound traffic: rising.

CPU spike: three hours ago.

Auth requests: inconsistent.

You're not investigating a breach.

You're living in one.

Already inside. Already seen.

What do you do next?

[30] Activate the Toolkit and Follow the Ronin Trail

You've passed the test. Now you join the real defenders.

[31] Destroy the USB. This Goes Too Deep.

This isn't your fight. You're not ready. Walk away before you're a target.

[32] Clone the USB, Send One to Legal, and Keep One Hidden

Play both sides. Build leverage. No one survives this alone.

[33] Hold It for Now—Wait and Watch

Timing is everything. Knowing when not to act is sometimes the real mastery.

Chapter 10

Plug the USB into a Sandbox Environment

You don't plug mystery drives into your daily workstation.

That's lesson one.

You retrieve your field laptop—a clean machine, air-gapped, un-trusting by default—and boot into a hardened sandbox environment you built years ago for malware triage and self-loathing weekend hobbies.

You've seen fakes.

Scareware.

Triple-staged honeypots dressed up as leaked admin tools.

This doesn't feel like any of them.

No Bluetooth. No clipboard. No dreams of safety.

Just cold, isolated silicon.

The USB clicks into place like a key into an old lock.

Nothing auto-runs. Good.

You open the drive manually. Inside:

- A single encrypted archive:

  RONIN_BLADE_V1.ZIP

- A SHA256 hash printed in the file title—pre-calculated and correct

- README.txt — the most ironically named file you've ever seen

  README.txt — RONIN INITIATION PACK

If you're reading this, your clearance was upgraded by circumstance—not by design.

Do not trust your logs. Do not trust your firewall.

The Phantom Firewall is not a misconfiguration—

It's an adversarial defense engine designed to mimic legitimate perimeter behavior

while leaking data beneath your IDS threshold.

This isn't just an attack vector. It's a sleeper framework, engineered to survive red team scans and board-level audits.

Contained in this package:

- Passive protocol anomaly detector

- Memory-bound heuristic scanner (no signature use)

- RONINTRACER: Extracts firewall rule deltas against synthetic test packets

- YAML file: firewall_truth.yaml — 147 encrypted hashes. Each labeled. Each timestamped. Possible collaborators. Or victims.

You pause.

This isn't a warning. It's a recruitment.

You scan the files using your local anti-malware tools. Clean.

But that doesn't mean safe.

You recognize fragments of what DeadClock warned you about—only now, it clicks. This USB didn't come from him. It came first. A test. His archive wasn't the trigger—it was the confirmation.

You check file behaviors in an isolated VM:

- No unexpected registry changes

- Network calls only attempt local pings

- One script tests DNS poisoning... against your own loopback

That's clever.

It's watching how you watch it.

You execute **RONINTRACER**.

The tool fires synthetic test packets against a mirrored version of your firewall rules.

Within seconds, it returns a delta report showing that the live firewall's behavior changes—based on who's asking.

You've caught lies in logs before—sloppy edits, replayed traffic, spoofed entries.

But this isn't hiding.

It's performance.

Tailored for the observer.

You're not hallucinating.

This thing isn't just adaptive. It's... aware.

"Run it, and you're in.

Walk away, and forget this ever existed."

— D

The final message prints:

"You're ready. You just don't know it yet."

The drive wipes itself—DoD standard.

No trace. Like it was never there.

Your forensics tool logs confirm it.

You sit in silence.

You've just been handed a toolset that proves a theory you weren't ready to believe.

You weren't sent to investigate the firewall.

You were chosen—because you'd be curious enough to look.

And now?

You're in it.

What do you do next?

[34] Access the Vault Location Listed in the YAML File

You have hashes. You have IPs. It's time to see what the Phantom Firewall was hiding.

[35] Check if Any Hashes Match Public CVEs

If this thing is weaponized, you need to know what it's targeting—or who.

[36] Refuse to Play the Game

This may be truth. Or it may be entrapment. And you're not playing.

[37] Broadcast This Finding to Your Red Team

Time to turn defense into offense. Bring in the warriors.

Chapter 11

Isolate the Firewall From the Network

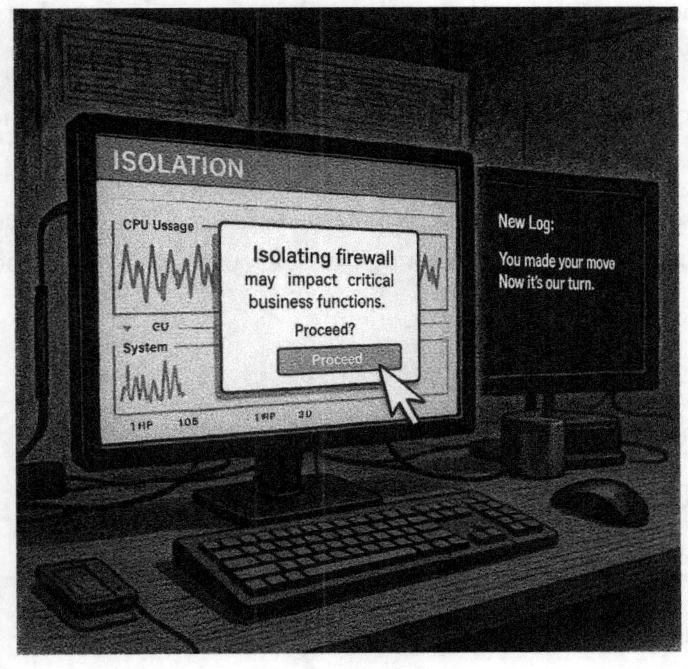

The firewall is no longer a line of defense.

It's not a barrier.

It's a character in the breach—an actor playing both sides, hiding its true role behind layers of protocol and illusion.

You've seen enough.

Your fingers move with the confidence of someone who's burned themselves before—someone who learned the hard way that decisive action is sometimes the only thing standing between a security event and a security incident.

You open the isolation console, hands hovering over the commands.

Every part of you is tense. Not fear of failure—but the weight of consequences. Alarms. Disruptions. Dependencies no one documented.

Isolation Sequence:

- Block external perimeter traffic

- Sever partner tunnels

- Redirect inbound to honeypots

- Freeze rule updates

- Snapshot + export config to offline vault

You pause before execution.

Because once you hit enter, there's no **"*oops*"** button.

Your monitor flashes a soft warning:

**"Isolating firewall may impact critical business functions.
Proceed?"**

You stare at the prompt.

The firewall itself seems to be asking the question.

As if daring you.

You smile. A small, tired, defiant thing.

"Proceed."

The commands fire.

Outbound connections plummet.

Tunnels collapse like paper bridges in a storm.

Your console lights up — **yellow, orange, red** — systems screaming in protest.

- "VPN concentrator dropped."

- "API gateway error — payment processing unavailable."

- "Partner SFTP sync failed — retry scheduled."

Your phone lights up with notifications. Slack. Email. SMS.

People are noticing.

The firewall logs go quiet. *Too quiet.*

Then a new entry appears in the console—one you didn't generate:

"You made your move. Now it's our turn."

And the CPU usage on the firewall spikes.

You check the system graph.

It's running processes you didn't authorize.

It's rebuilding.

Tunnels reappear. Hard-coded configs—ones you never approved—kick in like ghost limbs.

It's not panicking.

It's fighting back.

You lock the console.

Deploy a secondary layer of isolation—this time, severing the physical link at the switch level.

The port goes dark.

The heartbeat stops. ***Silence.***

For a moment, there's nothing.

Just the quiet hum of the SOC.

The sound of your own heartbeat.

Then... the first Slack DM arrives:

> **"What just happened? Why is production down?"**

You sit back.

You bought the company time.

Now you have to survive what happens next.

What do you do next?

[17] Go Rogue and Activate the Cyber Ronin Protocol

There are legends of a hidden defense program buried in the stack. Maybe this is why you were brought in.

[38] Check the Printer Output for Clues

If someone's been hiding config deltas, maybe they left a paper trail.

[39] Patch the Gaps and Restore

Time to clean up and restore, one connection at a time.

[40] Reboot the Firewall and Pray

Sometimes the simplest reset buys breathing room... or disaster.

Chapter 12

Ping a Red Team Contact for Help

Your hands hover over the console, sweat cooling on your palms.

You've bought time. *Barely.*

And in cybersecurity, time devalues faster than crypto in a crash.

You could go official.

But official means red tape. Official means chain of command.

Official means delays, politics, and "lessons learned" emails after the breach.

So instead, you reach out to someone who's not supposed to exist in this story.

Someone you met during a consulting gig at a Fortune 50, deep in the bowels of a red team exercise that got too real.

Contact: TofuBlade

A legend in offensive security circles.

Known for getting root on an air-gapped nuclear control simulator during DEF CON.

Known for once hacking a smart fridge at a CISO's house party—for fun.

Doesn't use their real name. Not even at DEF CON. Not even with friends.

You send the signal.

Not a message. **A beacon**.

A single DNS query, steganographically loaded—just enough entropy to raise a flag, but not a firewall.

Two minutes pass.

Your phone vibrates—old school SMS.

"Heya Ronin. What's the score?"

You reply:

"Phantom Firewall. Adaptive ruleset. Possible AI-enhanced. Insider fingerprints. Need a second set of eyes."

A pause.

"I'm in. Share a shell?"

You hesitate. Sharing access means shared risk. If they're compromised, so are you.

But this is what you called for.

You spin up a disposable container on your isolated network segment.

Send the creds.

TofuBlade connects within seconds.

"Whoa. This thing's not just alive," TofuBlade types.

"It's thinking. Behavioral mods. Real-time. Adapting like it knows we're watching."

"Did you notice it fingerprints admin consoles

and adapts its output?"

"Yep."

"And you let it run this long?"

"Had to confirm. Now what?" you ask, watching the packet logs pulse like a heartbeat.

"Now we see if it lies to both of us or just to you."

Together, you launch side–by–side queries from separate interfaces.

The firewall gives different answers to each of you.

Different ports open. Different rulesets apply.

TofuBlade whistles, low and impressed.

"Someone trained this. Someone funded this.

This isn't a script kiddie backdoor.

This is enterprise–grade deceptionware."

"Kagemusha?"

"Looks like. I've seen traces of it before—

in places where politics kept it quiet.

You sure you want to keep pulling on this thread?"

You stare at the screen.

You called them in.

You lit the signal.

What do you do next?

[41] Fortress of Packets

Clone the firewall config, isolate it in a sandbox, and dissect it before it notices you're watching.

[42] Ghosts in the Wire

If it adapts to identity, maybe you can spoof it. Or maybe it adapts to that too.

[43] The War Room Convenes

Call in the stakeholders. Build your allies now—before the breach goes public.

[45] The Red Team's Gauntlet

If it's a black box, maybe it's time to carve it open and see what bleeds.

Chapter 13

Keep Digging Into Logs

You sit back, eyes stinging from too many screens, too many dashboards—and too few answers.

The Phantom Firewall is adapting.

Your red team contact just confirmed it.

And leadership? They're either blind or complicit.

If there's truth to be found, it's buried in the logs.

Not in summaries. Not in alerts.

Not in the polished SIEM dashboards built for auditors.

Not in the filtered views meant for exec reports.

It's in the noise between the signals.

The raw, ugly, unstructured logs no one bothers to clean—because they assume no one's watching.

You pull up the syslog buffer.

Line after line scrolls by. Normal at first glance: port opens, closes, route confirms, health checks.

But you start to notice the inconsistencies.

- **Timestamp drift** — entries arriving before their parent processes should have existed

- **Source spoofing** — internal IPs making requests across non-routable or decommissioned subnets

- **Disappearing act** — sessions start and stop without any auth handshake logged

You cross-reference the log file sizes.

Too small.

Too clean.

As if something's scrubbing as it goes—erasing the echoes before they even reach disk.

Logs lie.

RAM remembers.

You pivot to cached RAM on your forensic VM.

There, buried in RAM remnants, are fragments of what the logs tried to hide.

Connection Attempt:

- **user:** svc_shadow_legal

- **dest:** \\DC-LEGACY01\ShadowLegal\2023-04\FinalBriefing.pptx

- **protocol:** SMBv1 (override)

- **note:** do not log

Your stomach drops.

Someone resurrected SMBv1 just long enough to copy out files, then re-disabled it before the system could even register the change.

This isn't a breach. This is a controlled extraction.

You search deeper.

You find entries marked as coming from your own machine—requests you didn't make.

At least, not knowingly.

The firewall isn't just watching. It's framing.

A final line of log text flashes on the screen, before the buffer clears itself:

"Good hunting, Ronin.

Let's see if you can find me before I find you."

You stare, heart pounding.

Whoever wrote that isn't afraid.

They're not chasing. They're playing.

And you're already on the board.

What do you do next?

[14] Ignore Orders and Declare an Internal Security Event

Pressure the system. See who reacts.

[19] Type INITIATE — Trigger the Hidden Protocol

Force the ghost to move. Trigger its next step.

[30] Activate the Toolkit and Follow the Ronin Trail

Use their blueprint. Walk their path.

[34] Access the Vault Location Listed in the YAML File

If you can find the archive, you can find the truth.

Chapter 14

Ignore Orders and Declare an Internal Security Event

Your cursor hovers.

The CIO's words blink back at you:

"Do not escalate. No panic."

They're not a suggestion. They're a warning.

But the breach isn't waiting for board approvals or carefully crafted press releases.

The Phantom Firewall is active, adaptive—and malicious.

And every second of hesitation is another second for it to learn, exfiltrate, or worse.

You draw a long breath.

Open the secure incident management console.

You choose to light the fuse.

Even if it burns everything down.

Declare Event: Level 1 Internal Security Breach

The form is short, but the weight is massive.

Your fingers move fast:

Event Type:

- Unauthorized network activity

- Suspected insider threat

- AI–assisted firewall compromise

Assets at Risk:

- Perimeter defense infrastructure

- DC–LEGACY01

- Privileged account integrity

Immediate Actions:

- Firewall isolated

- Containment initiated

- External connections severed

Priority: *Critical*

You hit **submit**.

And feel the world shift.

Within seconds, the automated response protocols fire:

- A notification hits all SOC, IR, and CIRT team members.

- The internal incident bridge opens—secure, logged, and now mandatory for senior tech staff.

- Partner systems ping with alerts about interrupted connections.

Your phone lights up.

The first call: **CIO**

You answer. Their voice is *cold but controlled.*

> **"Tell me you didn't just declare a breach**
>
> **against explicit instructions."**

You respond, steady:

"I did. And you'll thank me later. The firewall was lying to us.

It's behavioral. It adapts. It was leaking under threshold.

We're compromised."

There's silence. Then:

"I hope you're right.

Because that move just blew up the merger timeline."

Messages flood in.

Some are **angry**.

Some are **panicked**.

A few... **quietly grateful**.

But what matters is that the machine is moving now.

The company is no longer pretending.

You watch as incident handlers join the bridge, as isolation steps get double-checked, as logs begin to pour into forensic storage where they can't be scrubbed mid-flight.

And somewhere in that flood of data...

The Phantom Firewall watches.

And begins rewriting its playbook.

What do you do next?

[16] Call a Secret All-Hands with the SOC Team

If the leadership won't act, you'll rally those who will.

[30] Activate the Toolkit and Follow the Ronin Trail

If the Ronin left a trail... maybe it leads to the truth.

[43] The War Room Convenes

Secure your standing. The suits will need to choose a side.

[47] The Boardroom Firewall

Make it official. Blast the facts where no one can ignore them.

Chapter 15

Leak Sanitized Details to a Reporter

You declared the breach.

Quarantined the firewall.

Got ghosted by Legal.

Leadership? Full containment-spin mode. **Not incident response.**

And every instinct in you says: **if they could bury this, they would.**

This isn't revenge.

This is pressure.

You leak to force motion.

You open an encrypted session from your field laptop and route through a secure proxy chain—layered, randomized, untraceable.

Then you open your contacts list—not your corporate one.

Your real one. You scroll to an entry labeled:

"Signal: EchoPress // Infosec desk"

A reporter you met during an RSA afterparty two years ago.

She was the only one smart enough to ask the question no vendor dared answer:

"What's your breach detection average—

before you call legal?"

You shoot a message:

"Interested in a story about a learning firewall, a buried

insider, and a $2.3B merger hanging by a thread?"

The reply comes within 30 seconds:

"Anonymous or exclusive?"

"Anonymous. With artifacts."

You package what you can safely share:

- **Sanitized firewall logs** showing behavioral manipulation
- **Screenshots** of conflicting admin rule outputs
- **Evidence** of legacy credential resurrection
- **Redacted message**: "You're not ready."

You exclude hostnames, user IDs, client names—anything that could tie this directly to your employer.

And then, just before you send it, you attach a single line:

"If this makes the front page, the breach stops being internal."

Then you hit **Send**.

You sit still.

Ten minutes later, your internal Slack lights up.

"Did someone leak to the press?"

"How did EchoPress get our firewall screenshots?"

"Was this verified internally?"

"Why wasn't this escalated to the board first?"

The panic is louder than the silence ever was.

You smile.

The game has changed.

Now everyone's watching.

Now someone has to act.

A text arrives on your burner phone.

Unknown number. No name.

"You made the breach visible."

"That's one way to flush out a ghost."

"But now the ghost sees you too."

—R

What do you do next?

[54] The Story Beyond the Walls

Leaks reveal guilt faster than audits.

[55] The Shield Beyond the Walls

You made enemies. Time to protect yourself.

[56] The Vigil Never Ends

If transparency is your weapon—wield it fully.

[57] The Unseen Blade

The room's on fire. Step into it and lead.

Chapter 16

Call a Secret All-Hands with the SOC Team

You close the incident console, heart still racing.

The breach declaration stirred the pot.

The leak turned up the heat.

Now it's time to build a force that doesn't just observe—It responds.

The official IR team is tied up in politics.

The execs are shielding their careers.

But your SOC team?

Underpaid. Overworked. Ignored by the org chart.

But when things go loud? **They're ready.**

You send a message:

#SOC–HIDDEN–BRIDGE:⊠PRIVATE⊠MEETING⊠—⊠NOW.

If you know, you log in.

Within minutes, you see familiar names joining the hidden channel:

- **J3dEye** — log analysis wizard, keeps snacks in their server rack

- **PingQueen** — network pathing savant, once traced an internal phishing campaign back to the marketing team's own vendor

- **NullPanic** — junior analyst, but faster on a keyboard than most architects

You speak first. No slides. No hand–waving. Just facts.

> **"We've got an adaptive firewall, folks. Behavioral.**
>
> **It's learning us while we try to learn it.**
>
> **Someone planted it, and they're still active."**
>
> **"I don't care what the C–suite wants. I care what the**
>
> **network needs. We contain this now, or we let the**
>
> **ghost run the show."**

There's silence.

Then J3dEye types: **"About time someone called it."**

PingQueen adds: **"I've been seeing inconsistent ICMP responses all week. Thought I was losing it."**

NullPanic: **"Tell us where to point our tools."**

You lay out the plan:

Build a parallel logging pipeline

- Vault raw logs from compromised endpoints

Create synthetic admin accounts

- Bait the intruder into privilege traps

Deploy honeypots labeled as "Merger Critical"

- Track unauthorized access patterns

Monitor touchpoints in real time

- Trigger alerts on unexpected movement

The team gets to work.

Fast. Precise. No fear, no politics. Just action.

You watch the terminal scroll. For the first time, you're not alone.

The Phantom Firewall isn't the only thing adapting anymore.

Now it's not alone—

And neither are you.

What do you do next?

[58] The Network Yet to Come

Lure the ghost into the open—see how it moves.

[59] The First Stones of Tomorrow

The team has your back. Now brief the ones who sign the checks.

[60] The Shield Tested Together

Become the adversary the adversary didn't expect.

[61] The Coalition of the Willing

If this blows up, cover your tracks first.

Chapter 17

Go Rogue and Activate the Cyber Ronin Protocol

The bridge call fades behind you—voices arguing, analysts typing, execs panicking.

But you? You're calm.

Because while the breach is new, the moment isn't.

You've seen this pivot before—when **defenders stop reacting** and **start choosing their fight**.

You close the standard consoles, silence the alerts, and slide open a hidden partition on your field laptop.

A toolset you never mentioned during onboarding.

A toolkit that wouldn't survive procurement—let alone an asset inventory.

The Cyber Ronin Protocol.

You built it after your first burn.

After the breach no one talks about—the one that took down a healthcare giant for a week while execs lied on camera.

It's not flashy. It's not even elegant.

But it's yours. And it works.

You execute:

```bash
# Bash — Cyber Ronin Protocol Execution

./ronin_protocol.sh \

--scan    # Deep packet analysis

--trap    # Deploy synthetic decoys

--mirror  # Clone traffic to black-box vault
```

It begins:

- **Scan** — Deep packet inspection, signatureless anomaly detection, passive beacon trace

- **Trap** — Deploy decoy assets, emit false credentials, flood passive listeners

- **Mirror** — Real-time traffic clone to offline vault: yours, unlogged, unalterable

The network hums in response.

Your terminal glows with raw output—too fast for a normal analyst to follow, but your mind's already ahead of it.

The Phantom Firewall flinches.

Adaptive rules shift. Tunnels bloom open like false promises.

Syslog entries sprout—cover stories in real time.

But the Ronin Protocol doesn't read the logs.

It reads the truth beneath them.

Your screen flashes:

"UNKNOWN OUTBOUND SIGNAL DETECTED —

BEHAVIORAL MATCH: KAGEMUSHA"

"ROGUE☒PROCESS☒INITIATING☒SELF-MODIFICATION"

"ATTEMPTING TO WIPE TRACE — BLOCKED"

You've caught it.

Cornered it.

The Phantom Firewall just realized it's been unmasked.

And now it will fight back.

Your phone buzzes.

An encrypted message:

> **"You weren't supposed to see this. You're good.**
>
> **But are you ready?"**
>
> **"Blade Protocol, Phase 2. You're in it now."**
>
> **—R**

You lean forward.

The warmup's over.

The real battle begins.

What do you do next?

[62] The Day the Network Stood Still

Feed the firewall synthetic behavior—confuse its learning model.

[63] The Ronin Doctrine

When digital fails, go analog. Kill the cables.

[64] The Next Blade

No more secrets. Let the ghost know it's been seen.

[65] The Watcher Returns to the Shadows

Silence can be the sharpest blade.

Chapter 18

Type OBSERVE — Watch, Learn, Gather More Intel

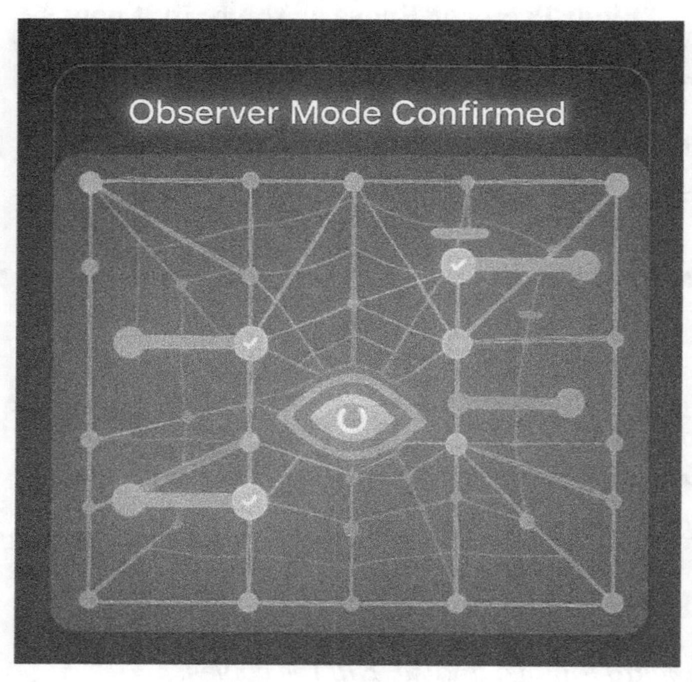

Your fingers hover over the keyboard, heartbeat drumming in your ears.

Your instinct wants to act. To fight.

But your training tells you: sometimes, *the sharpest blade is the one you don't draw*.

You type:

bash

> Command: OBSERVE

And press enter.

The terminal flickers. The prompt fades.

For a moment, the screen is black.

Then the world opens.

A hidden interface loads—one not designed for operators, but for architects.

A diagnostic console, raw and unpolished, filled with real-time data streams.

"This isn't the admin view.

It's the puppet master's."

Rows of logs scroll by—unfiltered, unredacted:

- Live exfiltration data, tagged and routed

- Adaptive rule changes triggered by simulated threat events

- Synthetic admin logins used to mislead auditors

You see traffic rerouted through shadow tunnels.

You see file hashes, packet sizes, session IDs.

You see the **blueprints of the deception**.

And then you see them: *A list of observer nodes.*

Endpoints in partner networks, cloud instances, remote offices—systems that have been **watching you** as you watched them.

Your screen updates:

"Observer mode confirmed.

Welcome to the real perimeter."

A map appears—your company at the center.

Radiating out: partner connections, supply chain networks, customer integrations.

Lines where data has flowed unnoticed.

Lines that form a web.

You've uncovered the Phantom Firewall's true function:

It's not just protecting. **It's mapping.**

Every connection. Every trust relationship. *Every blind spot.*

Suddenly, a new message appears:

"You chose to watch. That makes you dangerous."

"Remember: The first to see is the first to be seen."

Your packet monitor spikes.

Inbound traffic—targeted at you.

Pings, probes, crafted packets.

The Phantom Firewall is testing you now.

You lean forward, mind racing.

You have what you came for.

But now... ***You're part of the system.***

What do you do next?

[45] The Red Team's Gauntlet

Teach it the wrong lesson. See what it does when it thinks it's winning.

[66] A New Battlefield

You've seen enough. Don't give it a chance to learn you further.

[67] Echoes in the Mesh

Sometimes the best defense is hiding among the watchers.

[68] The Firewall Sleeps, But the Blade Remains

This is the proof no one could ignore.

Chapter 19

Type INITIATE — Trigger the Hidden Protocol

You stare at the blinking cursor.

You've watched long enough.

The map, the tunnels, the observer nodes—you've seen the web for what it is: **a machine built to learn, to hide, and to survive.**

But now? It's time to stop watching. It's time to act.

Your fingers move:

Bash

> Command: INITIATE

You hit enter.

The terminal freezes.

The laptop hums—like a storm building beneath your fingertips.

The screen flickers once, twice—then resolves into a command tree you've never seen before.

"RONIN BLADE PROTOCOL —

PHASE 2 UNLOCKED"

Commands appear:

- **/trapdoor** — Deploy a system-level honeypot that mimics a critical asset

- **/purgeghosts** — Force reset of adaptive rule history

- **/mirrorworld** — Duplicate all live network activity to a black–box vault

- **/severlink** — Burn all external tunnels, hard stop

Your heartbeat echoes in your ears.

This is no longer standard incident response.

This is cyber warfare, Ronin style.

You choose **/purgeghosts**.

The system responds with a warning:

"Executing this command will force the Phantom Firewall into recovery mode. Behavioral data will be lost. Adversary will be alerted."

You hit **confirm**.

Your network map begins to change in real time:

- Observer nodes blink out, as if yanked from the web

- Shadow tunnels collapse

- The firewall stutters, rules rewriting themselves in a desperate attempt to rebuild context

Then... silence.

The Phantom Firewall, for the first time, **stops adapting**.

You've blinded it.

Reset it.

Stripped away the one thing that made it dangerous: **memory.**

Your terminal displays a final message:

"Well played, Ronin. But this was only Phase 2.

Phase 3 belongs to the Architect."

Your screen goes dark.

And somewhere in the depths of the network, a new process stirs.

The Architect was watching.

Now they know your name.

What do you do next?

[20] Disconnect and Wipe All Traces — Clean Exit

This is deeper than you're ready for. No shame in regrouping.

[29] Call a Team War Room and Start Building Champions

The firewall was just the beginning.

[36] Refuse to Play the Game

No more secrets. Everyone sees the truth now.

[66] A New Battlefield

Sometimes survival is the smartest move.

Chapter 20

Disconnect and Wipe All Traces — Clean Exit

Your fingers hover over the keyboard, the terminal's glow reflecting in your eyes.

The map still lingers in your mind's eye: a web of connections, blind trust, and hidden tunnels that betrayed everything your company thought it secured.

But you feel it—the shift in the air, the invisible gaze of a system that has seen you.

The Phantom Firewall knows.

And if you stay connected, it will learn more.

You take a breath.

It's time to leave—not out of fear, but because this isn't your battlefield anymore.

You fought. You learned.

Now, **survival is the mission.**

Your hand hovers. One last glance at the terminal.

You initiate your exit protocol:

- **Terminate active connections** — RDP, admin shells, observer nodes

- **Scrub local cache** — DNS history, session tokens, artifact remnants

- **Trigger secure wipe of temp directories** — 7-pass overwrite, military standard

- **Disable wireless radios** — no accidental pings, no last traces

- **Shut down packet capture tools** — clean slate, clean conscience

The console flashes:

"Wipe in progress... 3%... 27%... 88%... 100%."

You unplug. Power down.

The silence arrives, but the weight doesn't lift—it just shifts.

The Phantom Firewall still exists.

The Architect still watches.

But you? You're no longer on the board—at least for now.

You step back from the desk, the faint hum of server fans and overhead lights filling the void left by your disconnection.

A single sticky note remains on your monitor—one you wrote for yourself long ago:

"The only perfect defense is knowing

when to leave the fight."

CLEAN EXIT: YOU SURVIVED, BUT THE GAME CONTINUES

Badge Earned: *"The Silent Ronin"*

Wisdom Gained: *"Even the sharpest blade must rest in its scabbard."*

Want to try another path?

[27] Blame an Automation Bug (Sort of True...)

Sometimes survival means pointing at the script and saying, "It did it.".

[29] Call a Team War Room and Start Building Champions

In every breach, there's a moment to lead. This is yours.

[36] Refuse to Play the Game

Enough shadows. Time to put names on paper and call it what it is.

[66] A New Battlefield

You've left no trace. No one knows what you saw—but you do. And you're not done.

Chapter 21

Screenshot Protocol

You pause, fingers hovering over the trackpad.

Your instincts scream that what you've uncovered — the Phantom Firewall's behavioral anomalies, the ghost tunnels, the traces of KAGEMUSHA — is too big, too dangerous to leave in volatile memory.

If the system adapts, if it wipes logs, if it frames you...**You need proof**.

For them. For you. For the moment when truth becomes your only defense.

You fire up your capture tools:

- **Full-screen captures:** admin consoles, terminal outputs, log traces

- **Divergent config snapshots**: rule mismatches, silent edits

- **Observer web:** partner tunnels, unacknowledged trust links

Each image, each file, encrypted locally and tagged with hashes for verification.

Next, the delivery.

You access your burner account — a secure inbox on a disposable domain, one you spun up during a freelance gig in the Balkans.

Air-gapped. Set to auto-destroy contents 30 days from receipt.

You compress the package.

Add a one-line note:

"If I vanish, this is my legacy. Trust no console."

You hesitate—just for a breath. Then click **Send**.

The files are in the vault now — beyond the Phantom Firewall's reach.

Beyond your employer's control.

Beyond even your own, should you fall.

Your terminal pings with a single new message.

Anonymous. No source.

"Clever. But now we both have insurance."

You sit back. Pulse steady.

Because now, even if you're erased—your truth won't be.

What do you do next?

[9] Ping Your Old Homeland Threat Response Contact

You have proof. Now force their hand.

[28] Undo Everything and Re-Risk the Environment

Someone else saw this coming too. Find them—before the enemy does.

[64] The Next Blade

Truth, filtered just enough to get attention without retaliation.

[67] Echoes in the Mesh

Disappear. Listen. Let the network tell you what's next.

Chapter 22

Pull the Plug and Run

The hum of the server room feels louder now, like it's echoing in your skull.

DC–LEGACY01 stands before you — ancient, humming, hiding secrets that weren't yours to uncover.

The sticky note flutters slightly in the breeze of the cooling fans:

"DO NOT TOUCH — Transition Testing —

Signed: OPS–R"

But you've touched.

You've seen.

And now the walls are closing in.

Your mind races through the possibilities:

- The Phantom Firewall adapting in real time

- The Architect watching from some shadowed perch

- The risk that every second you remain ties you closer to a breach that wasn't yours to start

Your hand reaches down.

You grip the power cable — thick, old, dust–coated.

You hesitate—just for a breath. Then, with everything you've learned weighing on your fingers, you yank.

The server whines down, its disks spinning to silence.

The whir of the fans slows.

The lights on the switch blink out one by one, like stars winking out in a darkening sky.

You grab your bag.

Your portable drive.

Your field laptop.

You don't look back.

You don't want to see if anyone's watching.

You don't want to see what wakes when DC-LEGACY01 finally sleeps.

You move fast.

Out of the server room. Up the stairs.

Through the side exit, away from the cameras you've long since stopped trusting.

You hit the street.

Breathe the night air — heavy with ozone, city grime, and the faint taste of victory or defeat.

You're alive. But what you unplugged wasn't just power—**it was a secret that refuses to stay buried.**

CLEAN BREAK: *THE GHOST LIVES ON*

Badge Earned: *"Ronin in Flight"*

Wisdom Gained: *"Not every battle ends with a victor. Some just end with survivors."*

Want to try another path?

[19] Type INITIATE — Trigger the Hidden Protocol

No more waiting. If you're in, go all in.

[27] Blame an Automation Bug (Sort of True...)

"System glitch." Two words that calm everyone. Even if they're a lie.

[29] Call a Team War Room and Start Building Champions

You panicked—but now you rally. Make it count.

[36] Refuse to Play the Game

That plug you pulled? It might've uncovered something real.

Chapter 23

Hide and Observe
Who Enters Next

The server room hums with the weight of secrets.

DC–LEGACY01 stands silent for now, its faint whine replaced by the soft tick of cooling metal.

You move without sound, sliding behind a stack of decommissioned firewalls piled like forgotten tombstones.

You crouch low, heart pounding, breath slow and measured.

The smell of dust, ozone, and old plastic fills your nose.

And then—footsteps.

Heavy. Deliberate.

The server room door creaks open.

A figure enters, silhouetted by the weak overhead light.

They move with purpose—no hesitation, no curiosity. Black hoodie. Gloves. Cap pulled low.

A small black case in one hand.

They walk straight to DC–LEGACY01, as if summoned.

As if they'd been here a hundred times before.

You watch as they kneel, pull out a slim device, and connect it to a hidden port on the side panel.

No hesitation. No fumbling.

This is muscle memory.

The console on the server flickers to life.

They type—fast, efficient, no wasted motion.

Your eyes catch a glimpse of the screen:

"KAGEMUSHA PHASE 2: INITIATE CLEANUP"

The fan speed increases, as if the machine itself is preparing for its final act.

The figure pulls a thin silver drive from their case, inserts it into the port, and waits.

Seconds feel like minutes.

Then the screen flashes:

"COMPLETE — ERASE TRACES —

TERMINATE NODE"

They unplug, slide the panel closed, and stand.

But they don't leave.

They pause.

Turn.

And scan the room.

For one breathless moment, their gaze seems to lock on your hiding place.

You freeze.

You've hidden from red teams, nation-state drills, even a physical pentest gone sideways in Prague.

But this?

This is different.

The figure tilts their head slightly.

And walks away.

You stay hidden until the footsteps fade.

Until the door creaks shut.

Until only the hum of the servers remains.

You exhale.

Your hands shake slightly—not from fear, but from adrenaline.

You just witnessed the architect of your breach.

And they didn't come to steal.

You realize now:

 you're not hunting the breach. You're surviving its cleanup.

What do you do next?

[10] Plug the USB into a Sandbox Environment

You don't know who they are. But they knew where to go.

[27] Blame an Automation Bug (Sort of True...)

Make a record. Get it on the radar—before it's rewritten.

[34] Access the Vault Location Listed in the YAML File

This place has secrets. And now, no one's watching you anymore.

[64] The Next Blade

Leave quietly. But not without leaving a trail behind.

Confront Them with Your Phone Recording

Your pulse roars in your ears.

Your fingers tighten around the phone in your pocket, the screen already recording—video, audio, anything to capture this.

The figure at DC-LEGACY01 moves with precision, sliding a sleek silver drive into the hidden port.

You know this is your moment.

You could stay silent.

You could let them vanish again into the shadows.

But some battles demand a stand.

You rise slowly, stepping from behind the stack of decommis–sioned firewalls.

Your voice cuts through the hum of cooling fans and the tick of fading servers.

"Nice case. Bet that trick's gotten you places.

Smile for the camera."

The figure freezes.

One gloved hand still on the server, the other on the drive.

They turn, slow, deliberate.

Their face is hidden beneath the brim of the cap and the edge of the hood, but you can feel their stare.

A long pause.

Then, they speak.

Calm. Controlled.

"You shouldn't be here."

You lift the phone slightly, thumb hovering over the emergency broadcast shortcut.

"Neither should you. But here we are."

They tilt their head, as if weighing their next move.

"That footage won't help you.

By the time you can use it, no one will care."

You keep your voice steady.

"Then I guess we'll both find out."

For a moment, you expect them to rush you.

Instead, they unplug the device, pocket it, and step back.

"You're good. Better than they said.

But this isn't your fight."

They glance at your phone one last time, then slip toward the door.

"Send that to whoever you want.

They'll still choose the merger over the truth."

And then they're gone—into the dim hallway, footsteps fading fast.

You lower the phone.

The recording is solid.

Proof.

But proof of what?

And will anyone care?

And you realize—**some ghosts don't run. They linger. Waiting for someone brave—or foolish—enough to stay.**

What do you do next?

[30] Activate the Toolkit and Follow the Ronin Trail

The press won't protect you—but they might protect the story.

[31] Destroy the USB. This Goes Too Deep

Go official. Get it on record. Let Legal take the heat.

[54] The Story Beyond the Walls

You won't make headlines—but someone out there will notice.

[66] A New Battlefield

Vanish now. Resurface only when the truth matters again.

Chapter 25

Trigger the Fire Suppression System

You hear the footsteps.

You see the figure.

You feel the weight of the room—heavy with secrets, charged with tension.

And in that heartbeat, you decide: chaos is the equalizer.

You don't need to win this fight.

You need to control the battlefield.

Your eyes flick to the wall panel:

FIRE SUPPRESSION OVERRIDE — CO2 FLOOD

Your hand shoots out.

You slam the emergency release, twist the locking cover, and punch the red button beneath.

The hiss begins instantly.

White gas jets from ceiling vents.

The lights flicker.

The room temperature drops as CO_2 displaces the oxygen.

Alarms scream — high, piercing, disorienting.

The figure at DC–LEGACY01 stumbles back, their hand yanking their device free.

They curse under their breath, words lost in the roar of the system's flood.

You drop low, moving fast along the edge of the racks, eyes burning from the chill and the chemical sting in the air.

The server room becomes a fog of vapor and chaos.

The hum of the machines warps beneath the suppression roar.

The figure vanishes into the mist — either retreating or regrouping.

You don't wait to find out.

You slip through the side door, heart hammering, lungs tight from the gas.

Alarms still blare behind you as you blend into the dim emergency lighting of the hallway.

You've bought yourself time.

You've blinded them.

And in the confusion, you didn't just buy time—**you rewrote the rules.**

What do you do next?

[6] Remote into DC–LEGACY01

You didn't come this far just to flee. Leave something behind.

[24] Confront Them With Your Phone Recording

If they want to hide it, you're going to show it.

[39] Patch the Gaps and Restore

Use the panic. Flip it into a full-blown escalation.

[66] A New Battlefield

You've done enough damage for now. Disappear before it spreads.

Chapter 26

Explain Calmly and Hold Your Ground

The alerts are flooding in.

Slack pings.

Emails with subject lines in all caps.

Phone calls vibrating your desk like a drumbeat of corporate dread.

"WHO KILLED SALESFORCE?"

"DASHBOARD DOWN. EXPLAIN NOW."

"IS THIS A DDOS? WHAT DID YOU DO?"

You sit back for a breath, feeling the storm swirl around you.

But your mind is clear.

You open the bridge line.

The faces appear—engineers, managers, directors.

Some angry. Some afraid. And you speak.

"Let's take a breath. Here's what happened, and why."

Your tone is steady. Your words are chosen.

"We had legacy accounts—hundreds of them—

holding privileged access.

Many tied to systems no one claimed.

Many that hadn't been used in years,

except by attackers or processes no one monitored."

"We purged them. Yes, it caused disruption. That's what happens when shadow dependencies aren't documented. But what I did today closed doors attackers could have walked through at any time."

"The outage? It's the cost of cleaning up a mess that's been growing for years. We can restore what's critical. We can rebuild what's needed. But the risk? That's lower now than it was an hour ago."

The bridge is quiet. Someone tries to speak, then stops.

You see it—the shift.

From anger... to processing... to respect.

The CIO leans in:

"Okay. Walk us through recovery. What's first?"

You nod.

The storm hasn't passed. But you're steering now. **And this time, they're listening.**

What do you do next?

[14] Ignore Orders and Declare an Internal Security Event

Hold the line—then bring in the lawyers to reinforce it.

[30] Activate the Toolkit and Follow the Ronin Trail

You've got the leverage. Time to turn tools into transformation.

[39] Patch the Gaps and Restore

Fix the fires first. Then we rebuild.

[47] The Boardroom Firewall

Not everything needs to be loud. Sometimes, power lives in the paper trail.

Chapter 27

Blame an Automation Bug (Sort of True...)

The Slack pings hit like hail on a tin roof.

The bridge line fills with voices—urgent, angry, confused.

> **"What happened to our accounts?"**

> **"Salesforce is down!"**

> **"Our pipeline's dead! Who authorized this?"**

Your screen lights up with messages stacked in threads, your name tagged again and again.

You exhale slowly.

It's not panic. It's not regret.

It's calculation.

You need the space to finish what you started.

And that means buying time.

Buying cover.

You unmute on the bridge.

> **"We had an automation policy trigger unexpectedly.**

> **It looks like a purge script misread the legacy**

> **account list and applied hard removals**

> **without a human confirmation step."**

> **"We're investigating root cause now.**

> **I'm prioritizing restoration of critical dependencies.**

We'll restore access where appropriate while maintaining security posture."

It's not a lie.

The script did exactly what you told it to.

The surprise? That it worked—in a network held together by political duct tape and legacy sin.

You see the tension shift on the call:

- Heads nodding.

- Eyebrows lowering.

- The anger dulling into problem-solving mode.

"Okay, that happens. Let's focus on recovery."

"What can we restore first?"

You guide them:

- Bring back customer-facing systems

- Keep dangerous legacy accounts dark

- Frame the next steps as stability measures

- Keep the Phantom Firewall's shadow out of this conversation

You muted the politics long enough to keep fighting the real fight.

You didn't lie.

But you didn't give them the full truth.

And for now?

That's what the mission needed.

But you can already feel the firewall watching the lie take shape.

What do you do next?

[14] Ignore Orders and Declare an Internal Security Event

They wanted silence. You're giving them a siren.

[26] Explain Calmly and Hold Your Ground

Sometimes the lie is cleaner than the truth. Especially when it's technically possible.

[31] Destroy the USB. This Goes Too Deep

If no one finds the evidence, maybe the problem disappears too.

[59] The First Stones of Tomorrow

If you're going down, make sure your replacement has something better to inherit.

Chapter 28

Undo Everything and Re-Risk the Environment

The calls, the messages, the pounding of angry feet down the hallway—They break through even your practiced calm.

The pressure is relentless.

Directors demanding immediate fixes.

Sales leads shouting about lost deals.

Partners pinging for explanations.

You tried to hold your ground.

But politics is the stronger force today.

You open the admin console.

You scroll through the purge log, the kill list of legacy accounts you eliminated in the name of security.

Each one a risk reduced.

Each one a door closed to attackers.

Each one now a bargaining chip for internal peace.

A flicker crosses your mind—That first message, the one that started it all.

"They're already in. You have 72 hours."

And now, you're unlocking the doors they used.

You pause.

You whisper to yourself:

"This is the cost."

And you begin restoring.

- You re-enable the service accounts that should have been buried years ago.

- You restore permissions to forgotten test systems tied to production dependencies no one documented.

- You re-establish trust relationships that once made attackers drool.

Your console pings with success messages:

"Account svc_temp_migration restored."

"Legacy trust to DC–LEGACY01 reinstated."

"Shadow API key reissued."

The Slack pings change:

"Salesforce is back up!"

"Pipeline running."

"Thank you!"

You exhale. But it feels hollow.

You didn't save the environment. *You saved comfort.*

And somewhere out there, the **Phantom Firewall smiles—**

not because it beat you.

But because **you opened the door again.**

Badge Earned: *"The Ronin Who Yielded"*

Wisdom Gained: *"Sometimes, saving the system means endangering it."*

Want to try another path?

[14] Ignore Orders and Declare an Internal Security Event

Rollbacks are risks too. Someone needs to say it.

[31] Destroy the USB. This Goes Too Deep

The easiest way to fix a mistake is to erase the evidence.

[59] The First Stones of Tomorrow

Even after surrender, you can still shape what's next.

[66] A New Battlefield

You gave them what they wanted. Now disappear—and wait for the failure.

Chapter 29

Call a Team War Room and Start Building Champions

You've felt the pressure.

You've seen the panic.

You've faced the ghosts in the machine.

Now? It's time to stop playing defense alone.

It's time to build your army.

You open the incident bridge—not the official one, but a new one.

You send the call:

"All hands. War room.

This is for the people ready to fix it, not spin it."

One by one, they join.

- The SOC analysts who've been drowning in false positives for years

- The engineers who tried to patch systems no one gave them time to understand

- The architects who saw the blind spots but got ignored

- The red teamers who've been warning of this day since they first broke a test environment

You speak, and the tension shifts.

"We're facing a living breach—

a firewall that learns us while we try to learn it.

A network compromised in ways

no audit ever dared reveal."

"I can't fix this alone. No one can.

But together? We flip the script—starting now."

You lay out the plan:

- Build real-time behavioral baselines — not what the SIEM says is normal, what is normal

- Spin up honeypots that match what the adversary is targeting

- Deploy deception assets to flush out insider hands

- Create a secure vault of clean truth — raw logs, packet captures, config snapshots, outside the Phantom Firewall's reach

- Document everything—clean, forensics-grade—so when the cleanup crew shows up, the truth's already archived.

The team responds.

Not with politics. Not with fear. **But with action.**

You see the spark in their eyes—the fire of purpose.

You're not alone anymore.

This isn't just containment.

It's the start of a movement.

The Phantom Firewall had the first move. ***Now it's our turn.***

What do you do next?

[33] Hold It for Now—Wait and Watch

Sometimes the best strategy is patience. Let the network talk first.

[45] The Red Team's Gauntlet

Break it before they do. Then fix it stronger.

[48] Into the High-Risk Zones

You've seen the gaps. Time to rebuild the walls, one trust boundary at a time.

[50] The Human Firewall

You can't patch people—but you can prepare them.

Chapter 30

Activate the Toolkit and Follow the Ronin Trail

Your screen glows—heavy with what comes next.

The Phantom Firewall's deception laid bare.

The Architect's shadow looming over your network.

And now—the Ronin Edge toolkit waits.

A gift from a ghost. A blade in the war behind the screen.

You execute:

bash

ronin_edge --trace --unmask --observe --mirror

The terminal hums to life.

Code cascades like a falling curtain:

- **Trace** — Every packet flow mapped in real time, watching for the anomalies, the covert tunnels, the data drip–feed

- **Unmask** — Stripping away obfuscation layers, forcing hidden processes to the surface

- **Observe** — Tracking adaptive rule changes as they happen, seeing the firewall try and fail to deceive

- **Mirror** — Copying all activity to your black–box vault, proof no one can erase

The Phantom Firewall reacts.

You see the rules mutate—**desperate, erratic.**

Ports that never existed before open and close in seconds.

Synthetic accounts flash into existence, then vanish.

But this time, nothing hides.

You see the true Ronin trail:

- A hidden service on an internal node acting as a command relay

- A set of behavioral signatures tied to specific admin console use

- A pattern of log wipes happening milliseconds before the event they erase

And then—the final piece.

A hard–coded tunnel—destination: a trusted partner's network.

Not an outsider. **An insider.**

The breach was never contained.

The Phantom Firewall was only one actor in a bigger play.

The stage is bigger.

The Architect isn't just watching.

They've been hosting the show.

What do you do next?

[9] Ping Your Old Homeland Threat Response Contact

You need someone off the books. Someone who's seen worse.

[10] Plug the USB into a Sandbox Environment

Don't trust it. Box it in and see what it tries to do.

[36] Refuse to Play the Game

This wasn't just misconfiguration. It was sabotage.

[37] Broadcast This Finding to Your Red Team

Sound the alarm. If anyone can crack this, it's your crew.

Chapter 31

Destroy the USB.
This Goes Too Deep.

You sit alone in the dim glow of your field laptop, the Phantom Firewall's secrets still fresh in your mind.

The USB sits on the desk—**a slim, innocuous object**, but you know what it represents.

Not just evidence.

Not just risk. **A beacon. A breadcrumb. A trap.**

A tether to a conspiracy that stretches beyond your organization, beyond your mandate, maybe beyond your ability to survive.

Your fingers brush the device.

Your pulse is steady.

Your mind is clear.

Not fear.

Just the hard-won wisdom of someone who's seen the brave fall—holding the truth too tightly.

You pull out your portable shredder.

Industrial-grade, designed for precisely this.

You slide in the USB.

The mechanism hums to life, the sound low, mechanical, final.

Plastic. Metal. Memory.

Reduced to shards.

You gather the remnants, scatter them between three different disposal bags.

Gone. Scrambled. Scattered.

The air feels heavier after.

You've just severed a link to the truth.

But you've also severed a link that could have led them to you.

You chose survival.

And in this moment, it was the right choice.

Your terminal blinks:

"No signal detected. No traceable artifacts.

Ghost status confirmed."

The digital battlefield quiets.

But the war hums on—just beyond your reach.

You didn't win. You just walked away unseen.

Badge Earned: *"The Silent Ronin"*

Wisdom Gained: *"Even truth has a blast radius."*

Want to try another path?

[14] Ignore Orders and Declare an Internal Security Event

They won't know what you destroyed—but they'll know you acted.

[28] Undo Everything and Re-Risk the Environment

Put it all back. Maybe that's enough to stop the bleeding.

[33] Hold It for Now—Wait and Watch

Let the system breathe. If it changes, you'll know you were right.

[66] A New Battlefield

Sometimes the smartest move is not being here when the questions start.

Chapter 32

Clone the USB, Send One to Legal, and Keep One Hidden

Your fingers hover over the USB drive.

It hums with potential—evidence, leverage, danger all rolled into one slim device.

Destroying it is safe.

Keeping it is reckless.

Cloning it? *That's a Ronin move.*

You boot your hardened imaging tool— an old-school utility—text mode only. *No frills. No logs. No snitches.*

- Full byte–for–byte clone of the USB

- SHA–256 hash check for integrity

- Two exact copies: one labeled **LEGAL_DROP**, the other **R_BLADE_INSURANCE**

You encrypt both with separate keys, store the passphrases in isolated secure notes, and disable all auto–sync.

The **LEGAL_DROP** copy is sent via your company's official secure evidence portal, wrapped in compliance red tape, timestamped, audit–logged.

It lands in Legal's hands.

Now they don't just know—they inherit liability.

The **R_BLADE_INSURANCE** copy?

That one goes to an external black-box vault you control.

Offline. Unlisted.

A graveyard for inconvenient truths—until the truth needs to rise.

Your terminal flashes:

> **"LEGAL_DROP RECEIVED 2025-06-17 21:43 UTC"**

> **"R_BLADE_INSURANCE STORED 2025-06-17 21:44 UTC"**

You lean back.

The game just shifted.

You're not just in the game anymore. You're holding the ace they don't know about.

The Phantom Firewall isn't the only one with a hidden hand now.

What do you do next?

[14] Ignore Orders and Declare an Internal Security Event

They told you to stay quiet. You didn't.

[17] Go Rogue and Activate the Cyber Ronin Protocol

They won't act. So you will.

[54] The Story Beyond the Walls

If the system won't listen, the world will.

[67] Echoes in the Mesh

Tuck the truth away. Someday, it'll matter again.

Chapter 33

Hold It For Now—Wait and Watch

The USB sits on your desk.

A simple device, but heavy with implication.

It hums in your thoughts—a key to truths too dangerous to reveal too soon.

Your instincts tell you: **act now.**

Purge it. Clone it. Expose it.

But your training—the part forged in the fires of past breaches, botched responses, and boardroom betrayals—whispers a different-ent path:

"Sometimes, the sharpest blade is the one you don't draw."

You disable your network connections.

Power down your analysis VM—too loud, too curious for what comes next.

Slide the USB into a Faraday pouch and lock it in your portable safe.

You sit in the quiet, listening to the hum of cooling fans and the distant thrum of a building still asleep to its own vulnerability.

You choose to observe.

- **You monitor the network**—watching for unusual probes, pings, pattern shifts

- **You set silent traps**—low-interaction honeypots, fake credentials, beaconed files

- **You tune into the pulse of the system**—who's asking questions, who's gone quiet

You let the USB sit—silent bait in a waiting trap.

Unplugged. Untouched.

But not unnoticed. **And you watch.**

As the hours tick by, the patterns emerge:

- A partner system suddenly pings your DMZ at odd hours

- An admin console logs a failed attempt from an internal subnet that should be dark

- The Phantom Firewall itself stutters once—just once—as if searching for something it lost

You note it all.

Every anomaly. Every hint of hidden hands.

Your patience sharpens your edge.

Badge Earned: *"The Shadow Ronin"*

Wisdom Gained: *"Not every victory is won in the first strike."*

What do you do next?

[17] Go Rogue and Activate the Cyber Ronin Protocol

Force their hand. If Legal won't move, make them.

[54] The Story Beyond the Walls

You warned them. Now the world needs to know.

[66] A New Battlefield

Protect yourself. It might be about to blow.

[67] Echoes in the Mesh

Let the silence speak first. Then act.

Chapter 34

Access the Vault Location Listed in the YAML File

You stare at the YAML file on your hardened field laptop.

A handful of lines—less config, more coded invitation:

- **Vault:** 10.47.201.9:8443

- **Key hint:** BladePhaser_hash

- **Notes:** OFFSITE // TRUST NO CONSOLE

Every part of you knows this is bait.

But you also know that walking away means living with unanswered questions.

And you didn't come this far to stop at the door.

You boot a clean VM—air-gapped in spirit, surgical in intent.

You connect.

The tunnel opens—secure, point-to-point.

The vault responds:

"WELCOME RONIN. PHASE 2 CONFIRMED."

Inside:

- **A repository of configs** — the true rules the Phantom Firewall ran, not the ones you saw

- **Behavioral models** — profiles of internal admins, mapped responses to test events

- **Outbound relay logs** — proof of data drip–fed out over months, maybe years

- **A list of known collaborators** — internal accounts, partner systems, even external vendors with anomalous traffic patterns

And at the bottom, like a whispered dare:

"ARCHITECT KEY INITIATED.

OBSERVER MODE UNLOCKED."

You've found the nerve center.

This wasn't where the Phantom Firewall was managed.

This is where it was ***taught to lie.***

But the system responds:

"Connection flagged.

Observer monitoring active.

Proceed or disconnect?"

You're not alone in here.

The Architect is watching.

What do you do next?

[4] Notify Executive Leadership

Take only what you need. Minimize your footprint.

[10] Plug the USB into a Sandbox Environment

If you're going in, go all the way.

[53] The Final Walls

There's no time left. Build the wall. Hold the line.

[67] Echoes in the Mesh

Truth is patient. Watch who blinks first.

Chapter 35

Check if Any Hashes Match Public CVEs

Your fingers fly across the keyboard, the glow of your hardened terminal bathing the room in cold light.

The YAML file lingers in your thoughts—hashes, configs, behavioral prints like echoes from a ghost.

Evidence that the Phantom Firewall wasn't just an anomaly... it was built on something known.

And now you need to know what.

You fire up your offline threat analysis rig—***air-gapped, patched by paranoia, fueled by caffeine and spite.***

You run the scan:

bash

cve_match --input=firewall_truth.yaml --mode=deep

The results crawl across your screen:

- Matches to CVEs that should have been patched years ago

- Legacy exploits leveraged not for entry—but for persistence

- Obsolete admin tools with known supply chain flaws—still lurking in prod, like digital asbestos

- A startling match to a zero-day rumor you'd dismissed as smoke last year—now very real

One entry stops you cold:

CVE-2019-357357: Behavioral bypass in adaptive firewall engines — exploit code signature match confirmed.

The Phantom Firewall isn't magic.

It's weaponized familiarity.

It knows the weaknesses because it was designed on top of them.

And at the bottom of your terminal:

> **"Partial hash match: classified CVE —**
>
> **embargoed. Access denied. Eyes only."**

You lean back. There's more.

But someone made sure no one can see it — **not even you.**

What do you do next?

[9] Ping Your Old Homeland Threat Response Contact

If anyone's seen this before, it's them.

[14] Ignore Orders and Declare an Internal Security Event

This isn't a coincidence. Time to go loud.

[30] Activate the Toolkit and Follow the Ronin Trail

If the hash is real, there's more behind it. Follow the trail.

[36] Refuse to Play the Game

If this was planted, someone inside knows.

Chapter 36

Refuse to Play the Game

The code scrolls by.

The evidence mounts.

The Phantom Firewall's secrets pile up on your screen—connections that should never exist, rules that shouldn't change themselves, a shadow system hidden beneath the one you were hired to defend.

You could keep playing.

Follow the Architect's trail.

Out-hack the hackers.

But your gut says no.

This is bigger than cat-and-mouse.

This isn't just a breach. ***It's a betrayal coded into the backbone.***

You open the secure reporting portal—one that skips middle management, skips politics, goes direct to Legal and Risk.

Your report begins:

- **Incident Type**: Suspected insider threat

- **Summary**: Evidence of unauthorized firewall behavior, adaptive rule manipulation, shadow tunnels to partner networks

- **Indicators**: Hashes matching embargoed CVEs, observer node map, rogue admin console behaviors

- **Risk**: Data exfiltration, regulatory non-compliance, supply chain exposure

You attach:

- Sanitized screenshots

- Config deltas

- A summary of your RoninEdge traces

You hit **SUBMIT**—and in that moment, choose truth over silence.

The response is instant:

"Receipt acknowledged. Do not discuss externally.

Incident response team mobilizing."

Your phone buzzes:

"We need you in a secure room. Now."

You know how this goes. Whistleblowers don't get medals. They get exits. **You exhale.**

The game is over—for you. For them, ***the reckoning begins.***

Badge Earned: *"The Whistle Ronin"*

Wisdom Gained: *"To expose a ghost, sometimes you must stop chasing shadows and turn on the light."*

This is one ending of your story.

Yet the Mesh remembers every move. Choose a different path, and another fate awaits.

[3] Scan the Firewall Configurations

Play by the rules—for now. Let the system work.

[9] Ping Your Old Homeland Threat Response Contact

If internal trust is broken, look outside the walls.

[66] A New Battlefield

You did your part. Now get clear before the fallout hits.

[67] Echoes in the Mesh

Protect yourself. Quietly.

Broadcast This Finding to Your Red Team

The evidence piles up on your screen.

The Phantom Firewall's secrets. **The observer nodes. The CVE match.**

All pointing to a breach designed not to be detected, *but lived with.*

You could keep this quiet. You could try to win the game solo.

But that's not how Ronin work.

And today, the Red Team isn't your adversary.

Today, **they're your army.**

You open a secure channel:

#RED–WAR–ROOM: ACTIVE THREAT HUNT

You broadcast:

- The behavioral anomalies in the firewall

- The observer map showing hidden connections

- The rogue process hashes

- The suspected insider patterns

- The CVE signature matches

Your message is clear:

"Team — this isn't a flaw. It's a feature—

engineered deception baked into the perimeter.

We need an adversary mindset now.

Find its blind spots. Break its game."

Within minutes:

- Scripts light up across test segments

- Replay attacks probe for rule manipulation

- Honeypots deploy with tempting artifacts

- Stealth scans map where the firewall fakes its truth

The **Red Team is unleashed**—and for once, they've got permission to **burn it all down.**

Your console fills with findings:

- Hidden tunnels collapsing under probe pressure

- Rule sets adapting then failing under synthetic admin accounts

- Unlogged outbound traffic surfacing in packet captures

It's bleeding. It's cornered. And now, for the first time — **it's afraid.**

Badge Earned: *"Ronin Commander"*

Wisdom Gained: *"A lone blade cuts deep—but a strike team dismantles the system."*

What do you do next?

[14] Ignore Orders and Declare an Internal Security Event

Keep it anonymous. But don't keep it quiet.

[26] Explain Calmly and Hold Your Ground

Document the truth before it's rewritten.

[47] The Boardroom Firewall

The board needs answers. You're ready to deliver them.

[53] The Final Walls

Don't wait for proof—lock it down now.

Chapter 38

Check the Printer Output for Clues

The digital battlefield hums around you—alerts firing, logs streaming, red team chatter filling the war room.

But something pulls at the edge of your focus.

The **printer**.

The old, neglected network printer tucked in the corner of the SOC—a relic from a time when people still wanted paper for their change logs and firewall reviews.

You glance over.

It hums softly, a green light blinking—ready but forgotten.

You step closer.

The tray holds a thin stack of paper.

Still warm. Someone printed these minutes ago.

Pages someone printed in the chaos and never claimed.

You fan through them.

- A firewall rule diff—real, raw, unfiltered. A printout that shows what the console should have shown but didn't.

- A session token dump. Unmasked. Someone logged privileged activity and tried to hide it digitally—but left the print job.

- A hand-annotated map of the network, with a shaky circle around DC-LEGACY01 and the words:

"Root of deception.

Do not trust console output."

Your pulse quickens.

The last page is a note. Handwritten. Sloppy.

> *"If you found this, you're closer than I ever got.*
>
> *They forged the console. But forgot the printer."*
>
> *—R*

You exhale.

Physical evidence.

The Architect owns the console, the cloud, maybe the boardroom. But not this printer. Not yet.

And now, in your hands, **the truth no one could scrub.**

What do you do next?

[11] Isolate the Firewall from the Network

Cut the connection. Lock it down.

[22] Pull the Plug and Run

It's too much. Get out now—before it gets you.

[31] Destroy the USB. This Goes Too Deep

You weren't supposed to see this. Burn it before anyone else does.

[33] Hold It for Now—Wait and Watch

Hold your ground. Let it make the next move.

Chapter 39

Patch the Gaps and Restore

The network crackles with the fallout of your isolation strike—silent tunnels, failed handshakes, broken dependencies.

The Phantom Firewall's adaptive rules lie broken, its shadow tunnels severed.

But in the wreckage, critical business services gasp for air—partners disconnected, apps failing, transactions stalled.

It's time to rebuild.

On your terms.

You open the config console—raw, direct, no orchestration layers to get in the way.

One by one, you review:

- Every B2B VPN

- Every trusted SFTP

- Every API gateway

- Every cross-domain link

You verify:

- Authentic endpoints only—no ghost IPs, no unregistered peers

- MFA enforced where it was missing

- Encryption standards elevated—no legacy TLS allowed

For each tunnel:

- You bring it up manually.

- You run integrity checks on the handshake.

- You monitor initial traffic for anomalies—no more hidden outbound drips.

The network begins to breathe again.

Slow. Controlled. Clean.

Slack lights up:

"Order API restored!"

"Data sync clean!"

"Thanks for jumping on this!"

But more than thanks—you sense something else.

The fear is fading.

The trust? Rebuilding.

This wasn't just a reconnection. **It was a cleansing.**

Badge Earned: *"The Network Reforger"*

Wisdom Gained: *"Every connection is a risk—until you remake it with purpose."*

What do you do next?

[8] Run a Containment Playbook

Don't wait for another breach. Shut the doors now.

[14] Ignore Orders and Declare an Internal Security Event

Make it official. Start the process before someone else spins it.

[15] Leak Sanitized Details to a Reporter

Quiet isn't working. Time to go public—carefully.

[33] Hold It for Now—Wait and Watch

Give it a minute. Watch. Let the network breathe.

Chapter 40

Reboot the Firewall and Pray

The cursor blinks on your console like it's mocking you.

You've tried patching. You've tried tracing. You've tried containment.

But now? You're tired. You're out of time.

And sometimes the only move left is the dumb one.

You issue the reboot.

No shutdown procedure. No maintenance window. Just a raw, unceremonious hard kill.

For a moment—**silence.**

Then the fans spin down. The firewall's heartbeat dies.

A second later—lights flicker. BIOS wakes up like a hungover ghost.

And then?

Everything goes wrong.

The reboot process halts.

A new message appears:

"SYSTEM RESTORE FAILED -

CONFIG FILE INTEGRITY COMPROMISED"

"Attempting fallback to Ronin-Bypass-Protocol v1.04..."

"Fallback successful. Network state: UNKNOWN"

"Console user identified: RONIN_PROBATION"

You freeze.

Fallback? **To what?**

You pull logs. The bootloader skipped standard configs and loaded a backup image—one labeled with a timestamp that predates your hire date.

You didn't even know this version existed.

Connections start blinking alive—selectively.

- The vendor tunnel re-establishes—despite being disabled yesterday.

- Legacy partner connections flare up—routing through "trusted" circuits you flagged last week.

- A dev server in a "dark" zone starts issuing DNS requests in a pattern that looks... rehearsed.

Your EDR dashboard lights up.

- One alert: **"New parent-child process spawn from SYSTEM with unsigned runtime: ghost_init.sys"**

- Another: **"External sync detected with shadow-recorded rule stack."**

You blink once. Twice.

You didn't reboot the firewall.

You woke it up.

And now it's cleaning up after itself.

The screen refreshes once more, revealing a trailing comment at the end of the fallback log:

"Last edited by: Architect // Phase 3 readiness assumed."

A chill prickles your spine. This wasn't recovery. This was pre-meditated return.

You reach for the console again—but the CLI locks.

Your access is revoked mid-session.

On a separate monitor, a window opens:

"You tried to end the story.

But some firewalls don't reboot. They evolve."

Then the screen goes dark.

Just your reflection. And the hum of something alive in the background.

You tried to reboot the firewall. **It rebooted you.**

What do you do next?

[41] Fortress of Packets

Wrap the network in steel and pray it holds.

[42] Ghosts in the Wire

You see movement—but no one's admitting to it.

[43] The War Room Convenes

You'll need more than a reboot to survive this. Call the crew.

[45] The Red Team's Gauntlet

If you can't trust it, attack it. Find what breaks.

Chapter 41

Fortress of Packets

The network breathes.

But you know better than to trust the calm.

The Phantom Firewall's twisted rules are gone, but its shadow still lingers — in forgotten configs, in outdated certs, in interfaces left too open for too long.

You move with purpose.

No shortcuts. No assumptions.

Only clarity.

Only control.

Your console becomes your forge:

- **Tighten ACLs** — no more "temporary" rules that out-stayed their welcome

- **Restrict management interfaces** — no external access without explicit, logged approval

- **Rotate keys and certs** — the old ghosts won't find a foothold

- **Purge unused accounts** — no orphaned credentials left behind

Each change locks the foundation tighter.

Layer upon layer.

A fortress built, packet by packet.

The network map updates:

- Core services stable

- Trusted partners online

- External probes deflected cleanly

Your SOC chat lights up:

"Firewall baselines clean."

"Zero anomalies last scan."

"App latency back to normal — nice work!"

But you don't celebrate.

Not yet.

You feel it—the adversary watching, waiting for complacency.

You won't give it to them.

Badge Earned: *"Guardian of the Core"*

Wisdom Gained: *"A network hardened in haste invites regret. A network hardened in resolve commands respect."*

What do you do next?

[26] Explain Calmly and Hold Your Ground

You've got the logs. Now make the case.

[42] Ghosts in the Wire

Just because it's quiet doesn't mean it's over.

[44] The Hardened Baseline

If you want peace, build rules like they're walls.

[45] The Red Team's Gauntlet

If it holds against them, it'll hold against anything.

Chapter 42

Ghosts in the Wire

The core is stable. The tunnels are clean. **Services breathe again.**

But you know better.

Phantoms don't vanish without leaving shadows.

You scan the network map.

You don't see tunnels anymore—

You see potential hiding places.

Silent corners where remnants could wait.

Logic bombs. Backdoors.

Triggers disguised as normalcy.

You pivot fast:

- **Deploy forensic scans across core routers and firewalls** — every rule, every exception, every ghost

- **Sweep endpoint configs** — unauthorized scripts, odd scheduled tasks, unfamiliar binaries

- **Comb through DNS and proxy logs** — no outbound beaconing escapes your scrutiny

Then—patterns emerge.

- A harmless-looking cron job on a forgotten server

- A low-frequency DNS query—subtle, persistent

- A still-active service account tied to a long-retired app

You act without hesitation:

- **The rogue job** — wiped, logged, alert sent

- **The DNS beacon** — sinkholed, traced, reported

- **The account** — disabled, audited, root cause opened

The network map updates again:

- No anomalies detected

- No unexplained outbound flows

- No suspicious account activity

Your SOC chat lights up:

> **"Threat hunting complete — clean slate."**
>
> **"Nice catch on that DNS exfil stub —**
>
> **could've gone unnoticed."**

But you don't relax. This isn't victory.

It's vigilance. **Ghosts always try to return.**

Badge Earned: *"Hunter of Shadows"*

Wisdom Gained: *"A system can be rebuilt in hours. Trust takes longer — and constant defense."*

What do you do next?

[17] Go Rogue and Activate the Cyber Ronin Protocol

You've played the ghost. Now become the storm.

[54] The Story Beyond the Walls

Some threats need sunlight—but not too much.

[66] A New Battlefield

Disappear. But not forever.

[67] Echoes in the Mesh

If it adapts to identity, maybe you can mislead it.

Chapter 43

The War Room Convenes

The Phantom's ghosts are gone—**for now**.

But the true battle begins here:

Clarity. Alignment. Resilience.

You ping the core teams:

- Network Engineering

- Application Security

- Cloud Operations

- Business Owners of the Most Impacted Services

"Ten minutes. War room. No optional attendees."

The virtual room fills fast.

Faces. Names. Ranks.

Some hardened by fire.

Some pale from the fallout.

The chatter dies as you step in.

The Ronin's voice is calm. Clear. Controlled.

"We've contained the Phantom.

We've rebuilt. We've hunted.

Now we ensure it never happens again."

You lay it down with precision:

- **Timeline of the breach** — how the Phantom wormed in, how it spread

- **What was broken** — the tunnels, the rules, the trust

- **What was rebuilt** — clean routes, hardened systems, anomaly-free baselines

- **What was exposed** — orphaned accounts, config drift, trust assumptions

Silence.

Then nods.

The shared understanding forms—hard-won, but real.

Then comes the turn:

Next Steps

- Define and lock a hardened network baseline

- Accelerate segmentation and Zero Trust rollout

- Validate with live-fire red team ops

- Refresh incident response playbooks

- Train. Drill. Document. Repeat.

Someone speaks up—quiet but firm:

"Let's not waste the rebuild.

Let's use this to set a new standard."

And just like that, the war room becomes a forge.

Plans take shape. Ownership is claimed.

The future begins—this time, with eyes wide open.

Badge Earned: *"Strategist of the Rebuild"*

Wisdom Gained: *"Technology can be patched. Teams must be forged."*

What do you do next?

[36] Refuse to Play the Game

The time for whispers is over. Escalate officially.

[44] The Hardened Baseline

It's time to translate lessons into locked-down defense.

[45] The Red Team's Gauntlet

If it's a black box, break it open. Let the Red Team run wild.

[48] Into the High-Risk Zones

Some parts of the network are too risky to trust. Explore, isolate, survive.

Chapter 44

The Hardened Baseline

The war room fades from your screen—

but the momentum remains.

Words were easy.

Now comes the work.

You face the console.

Not for containment.

Not for combat.

But for doctrine.

Your mission:

- Capture the hard-won lessons
- Define "secure by design"—not as a slogan, but as **code, config, default**
- Make it real. Make it durable. Make it enforceable.

You begin with the pillars:

Access Control

— Least privilege is not optional

— No admin accounts without justification and multi-layer approval

Segmentation

— No flat networks

— No location-based trust

— Every zone is a castle with its own drawbridge

Encryption

— End-to-end, everywhere

— No legacy TLS

— No fallback modes

Visibility

— Every route. Every exception. Every privilege

— Logged. Reviewed. Justified

— No more "temporary" changes that rot into permanent risk

Your baseline grows—line by line:

- **Clean, enforceable rules** — no fluff, no hand-waving

- **Config templates** — firewalls, routers, proxies, identity stacks

- **Monitoring standards** — what's normal, what's signal, what's fire

The draft circulates.

Feedback comes fast:

> **"Let's integrate this into change control."**

> **"Can we bake this into CI/CD for infra as code?"**

> **"We need to align vendor SLAs to these standards."**

You nod.

This isn't policy. This is foundation.

And you're watching your team lay bricks in real time.

Badge Earned: *"Architect of Standards"*

Wisdom Gained: *"A network without a baseline is a castle without a blueprint."*

What do you do next?

[26] Explain Calmly and Hold Your Ground

Translate defense into documentation. Make it real.

[45] The Red Team's Gauntlet

If it fails now, it was never ready.

[50] The Human Firewall

The system's hardened. Now teach the people behind it.

[51] The Council of Resilience

The walls are up. Now win support from those outside them.

Chapter 45

The Red Team's Gauntlet

The plans are drawn.

The walls are built.

The baselines are etched in policy and config.

But paper defenses stop no one.

And you know better than most.

If the segmentation is to stand, it must be tested—

ruthlessly, creatively, relentlessly.

Before an adversary finds the cracks,

you'll send in those trained to break trust by design.

You summon the Red Team.

No tabletop games. No sanitized drills.

This is a **live-fire test** of your future.

The gauntlet is thrown:

- **Challenge segmentation at every layer** — from stubborn legacy apps to undocumented API whispers

- **Attempt lateral movement via compromised identities** — if a phished user pivots, what do they touch?

- **Hammer the boundaries** — from dusty firewalls to flashy SDN gates to cloud edge facades

- **Stress the visibility stack** — can the SOC see, correlate, and contain in real time?

The Red Team grins—hungry, respectful, ready.

They vanish into their digital armory.

And the war begins.

Your console lights up:

- Blocked probes at microsegment edges

- Unauthorized API calls — flagged, neutered, contained

- A low-tier legacy server—popped, but isolated, with nowhere to pivot

Every alert tells a story.

Every test refines the wall.

- **Automation gaps?** Tightened.

- **Documentation holes?** Filled.

- **Shadow dependencies?** Mapped and neutralized.

The test ends. The Red Team reports:

"Your walls held. We found flaws —

and you patched them faster than we could pivot.

If the Phantom returns, it won't find easy prey here."

Your console refreshes—

quietly, almost an afterthought.

Architect log sync request: **DENIED**

Resilience threshold exceeded.

Monitoring continues.

You nod. Not with pride.

But with readiness.

Badge Earned: *"Phantom's Bane"*

Wisdom Gained: *"The strongest walls are the ones you try to break yourself."*

What do you do next?

[46] Rewrite the Response — The Playbook Reforged

Old playbooks fail. New muscle memory must take their place.

[47] The Boardroom Firewall

You asked for pressure. Now show what cracked.

[51] The Council of Resilience

Resilience isn't a report—it's a coalition. Time to join it.

[66] A New Battlefield

You've seen enough. Sometimes the best move is quiet influence.

Chapter 46

Rewrite the Response — The Playbook Reforged

The Phantom taught you many lessons.

The Red Team proved them.

Now comes the harder part: **making sure those lessons don't fade in the quiet.**

You gather the core response leads:

- SOC Operations

- Forensics

- Engineering

- Business Continuity

- Comms and Legal

"Forget the old playbooks," you say.

"They were built for a flat network that no longer exists.

We respond now the way we rebuilt—

segmented, hardened, aware."

Together, you dismantle the outdated:

- **Flat response zones** — no more assuming tier-wide access

- **Implicit trust** — every responder authenticates, every action logs

- **Generic IR flows** — replaced with system-specific guides for each segment and platform

Then, you forge the new:

- **Microsegment-based containment** — respond without endangering adjacent systems

- **Identity-driven triggers** — stop lateral movement at the user level

- **Hybrid IR integration** — cloud or on-prem, response is seamless

- **Red Team learnings codified** — lateral movement, shadow APIs, credential traps

Plans become muscle memory:

- **A finance platform compromise** — caught at the boundary, restored in minutes

- **Cloud key abuse** — flagged by behavior, terminated before damage

- **A rogue dev board phones home** — trapped, sinkholed, traced

Exercises end.

No chaos. No panic.

Just clarity. Just control.

Your team doesn't just look ready.

They are.

Your terminal blinks softly in the corner:

"Last playbook update:

Architect access revoked."

"Phase 3 resilience assumed."

Badge Earned: *"Master of Response"*

Wisdom Gained: *"A network's strength is tested in battle, but proven in recovery."*

What do you do next?

[26] Explain Calmly and Hold Your Ground

Frame the narrative before someone else does.

[47] The Boardroom Firewall

You've uncovered the truth. Now it's time to show it upstairs.

[53] The Final Walls

The damage is real. Rebuild with intent.

[66] A New Battlefield

Sometimes it's safer to vanish—with the truth in hand.

Chapter 47

The Boardroom Firewall

The SOC is quiet now.

The tools are sharper.

The team stands ready.

But one more defense must hold—

The firewall of executive alignment.

Without it, everything you rebuilt can be undone by shifting budgets, diluted focus, or post–incident amnesia.

You don't bring fear.

You bring a story—

Forged in fire. Hardened in truth.

The room fills:

- **CEO** — reading between business risk and brand trust

- **CFO** — weighing exposure against spend

- **COO** — listening for impact to continuity and operations

- **Board liaison** — eyes on governance, reputation, and liability

You open not with slides, but clarity:

> **"The Phantom Firewall wasn't just an attack—**
>
> **it was an audition. It exposed how quickly**
>
> **we could have lost trust, revenue, and control."**

Then you walk them through the evolution:

What Changed:

- **Hardened baselines** — no more drift, no blind inheritance

- **Zero Trust segmentation** — attackers suffocate on entry

- **Playbooks** — live-tested, precise, repeatable

- **Defense posture** — independently validated under pressure

What It Meant:

- **Time to contain**: cut by 60%

- **Attack paths**: reduced to isolated zones

- **Visibility**: now proactive, not reactive

Then — the ask. Not funding, but **shared resilience**.

"We don't need permission. We need partnership."

- Endorse Zero Trust as a mindset, not a line item

- Fund red team validation as continuous hygiene, not emergency spend

- Align cyber risk to business continuity — not after the breach, but before

Silence.

Then questions — pointed, respectful.

You answer with calm confidence.

And then... nods.

Agreement.

Support.

The final firewall holds.

And this one defends not ports or packets—**but progress.**

Badge Earned: *"Champion of Resilience"*

Wisdom Gained: *"Technology defends. Culture endures."*

What do you do next?

[51] The Council of Resilience

Real change starts with resilience — and you've got a seat at the table.

[53] The Final Walls

The board listened. Now it's time to act.

[64] The Next Blade

Pass the torch. Shape the legacy.

[66] A New Battlefield

Sometimes surviving means knowing when to walk.

Chapter 48

Into the High-Risk Zones

The boardroom firewall held.

The support is secured.

Now comes the true test: **action.**

Zero Trust is no longer a theory.

It's a commitment—one that must be enforced where risk runs deepest.

You face the network map—your digital battlefield. Hardened. Scoured. Tested.

And still...

Your eyes lock on the zones that haunt you most:

- Core financial systems

- Customer data platforms

- Third-party integrations

- Legacy applications held together by duct tape and denial

You don't rush.

Zero Trust done right isn't a sprint—it's **precision warfare.**

You outline the plan:

- **Phase 1: Contain** — wrap each zone in segmentation; every connection starts as guilty until proven clean

- **Phase 2: Enforce** — identity at every checkpoint; no ACL approved without a business owner standing behind it

- **Phase 3: Monitor** — behavioral telemetry at depth; alerts tuned to whisper when things feel off

- **Phase 4: Refine** — configs evolve, gaps close, trust gets earned one rule at a time

The work begins:

- Firewall policies rebuilt

- Forgotten tokens burned

- Service accounts reviewed line by painful line

- Traffic traced, mapped, and validated live

The SOC watches.

- Unauthorized connections: zero

- Service uptime: stable

- Anomalies: seen, stopped, studied

What were once open plains are now defensible ground.

No longer soft targets. Now hardened zones.

And in the silence that follows, you feel it:

> ***The Phantom would find no easy prey here now.***

Badge Earned: *"Defender of the Crown Jewels"*

Wisdom Gained: *"Zero Trust isn't a product. It's a promise kept in every connection."*

What do you do next?

[47] The Boardroom Firewall

The board needs to know exactly what you walked into.

[49] The Unending Siege

Walls hold today, but vigilance decides tomorrow.

[51] The Council of Resilience

If this risk is systemic, it needs strategic leadership.

[53] The Final Walls

No more flexibility. Time to wall off what matters.

Chapter 49

The Unending Siege

The high–risk zones are fortified.

The segmentation holds.

The network hums — clean, contained, resilient.

But you know better.

Defense is not an achievement.

It's a mindset. A rhythm. A siege that never lifts.

If the Phantom taught you anything, it's this:

Complacency is the true breach.

You move quickly — no waiting for audits, no trusting quarterly dashboards to keep you safe.

The order goes out:

- **Red Team Cycles** — unscheduled, unsparing, unpredictable

- **Continuous Validation** — agentless scans, behavior analytics, attack simulation, API fuzzing — all 24/7

- **Telemetry Baselines** — updated in real time; anomalies surfaced before they whisper

Your team doesn't just watch. **They hunt.**

- A synthetic credential theft triggers a multi-factor lockdown

- Lateral movement dies at the segmentation line — no path forward

- A rogue API call is blocked mid-packet, quarantined, and traced back to its source

The Red Team sharpens its claws with every cycle.

Your defenses answer in kind — evolving, adapting, holding.

You establish the rhythm:

- Test

- Analyze

- Refine

- Repeat

The Phantom may rise again.

But when it does, it'll meet a network that doesn't wait.

That doesn't hope. **That prepares.**

Because this time, the shadows aren't hunting the defenders.

The defenders are watching the shadows.

Badge Earned: *"The Eternal Watcher"*

Wisdom Gained: *"Resilience isn't a goal. It's a habit."*

What do you do next?

[35] Check if Any Hashes Match Public CVEs

If these tunnels match known threats, you'll know who you're facing.

[47] The Boardroom Firewall

This is bigger than misconfiguration. They need to see it.

[66] A New Battlefield

Some tunnels weren't meant to be found. Leave no trace.

[67] Echoes in the Mesh

You don't need to act yet—just listen and log.

Chapter 50

The Human Firewall

Your network stands stronger.

Your defenses adapt daily.

Your architecture — forged through fire — is battle-tested.

But one truth remains.

And it hums louder than any alert:

The strongest defenses fail when human judgment falters.

The Phantom exploited config gaps, yes — but it thrived on human habits.

A clicked link.

A reused password.

A rogue app, installed ***"just to make things easier."***

If Zero Trust is to endure, people must live it.

So you shift focus.

Not to policies.

Not to dusty LMS modules.

But to human readiness.

You build a new blueprint:

- **Tailored Learning** — Devs study secure APIs. Finance sees fraud-simulated phish. OT staff walk through ICS-specific threats.

- **Interactive Tabletop Exercises** — From helpdesk to execs, every team makes real decisions in real-world drills.

- **Microlearning Moments** — Five-minute bursts, delivered when they matter most.

- **Simulated Threats** — Fake phish, rogue USB drops, mobile smishing — teach through tension.

- **Feedback Loops** — Failures refine the program. Wins become stories to share.

And slowly, you see it:

- Fewer clicks.

- More alerts filed.

- Conversations that begin with, "How do we close this?" — not "Do we need to worry?"

Your network has walls.

Your firewalls have rules.

But now — **your people know how to hold the line.**

Badge Earned: *"Builder of the Human Firewall"*

Wisdom Gained: *"Technology protects the network. People protect the mission."*

What do you do next?

[26] Explain Calmly and Hold Your Ground

Write it down. Institutional memory is your best defense.

[47] The Boardroom Firewall

The board needs to know the human firewall still has cracks.

[51] The Council of Resilience

You can't patch people—but you can prepare them.

[66] A New Battlefield

You've trained them. But that doesn't mean they'll listen.

Chapter 51

The Council of Resilience

You've built the walls.

You've forged the tools.

You've armed the people.

But resilience isn't solo work.

It's not a platform.

It's not just a policy.

It's a commitment — **shared, visible, constant.**

And that's why today...

You don't convene a meeting.

You forge a council.

The invitations go out:

- *Security leaders* — to ensure defense isn't a last–minute bolt–on

- *IT architects* — to bake resilience into every design

- *Operations* — to ground it in mission and uptime

- *Risk managers* — to map dollars to duty

- *Business owners* — because no app secures itself in a vacuum

The first session is quiet.

Titles mix. Silos bristle.

Old reflexes whisper:

> **"This is security's job. Not ours."**

You break that spell.

> **"This is shared resilience.**
>
> **The Phantom didn't just attack firewalls.**
>
> **It attacked our business, our customers, our trust.**
>
> **And defense is now everyone's business."**

You lay out the foundation:

- **Quarterly reviews** of key risks, readiness gaps, and actual incidents

- **Joint ownership** of uptime, recovery time, and supply chain integrity

- **Clear escalation paths** — no more crisis chaos

- **Business-aligned metrics** — not just patches, but impact avoided

- **Integration with board reporting** — resilience as a core KPI

It starts slow.

But then:

A nod.

A volunteer.

A question that bridges two silos.

And just like that —**The council forms.**

Not as a taskforce.

But as the network's final control layer:

Unity.

Badge Earned: *"The Unifier"*

Wisdom Gained: *"Resilience thrives where silos fall."*

What do you do next?

[26] Explain Calmly and Hold Your Ground

Without documentation, it'll happen again.

[52] The Trial of the Council

A council untested is a castle unstormed. Forge resilience in fire.

[64] The Next Blade

The mission outlives you. That's how you win.

[66] A New Battlefield

You gave them the tools. But that doesn't mean they'll use them.

Chapter 52

The Trial of the Council

Words forge plans.

Drills forge readiness.

The Cyber Resilience Council stands — diverse, committed, aligned.

But a council untested is a castle unstormed.

And storms don't wait.

You propose the trial: (*A full-scale cyber resilience exercise*)

- **no notice**

- **no exemptions**

- **no soft punches**

The council agrees.

The date remains secret.

Only you and a handful of shadow planners know what's coming.

Then it hits.

- **A simulated supply chain breach** — malicious code rides in via a trusted integration.

- **A critical SaaS outage** — customer access severed.

- **A targeted phishing attack** — a senior exec's credentials stolen and leveraged against finance.

But the network doesn't panic, it moves.

- **The SOC isolates the poisoned integration** — fast and clean.

- **BCP activates fallback systems** — operations barely flinch.

- **Identity team disables the compromised account** — privilege denied, forensics triggered.

- **The council assembles** — no blame, no confusion. Just clarity.

Decisions made.

Actions taken.

Trust earned.

When the drill ends, the silence is electric.

Not relief, **Readiness.**

The debrief hums with purpose:

- Time to detect: **improved.**

- Time to contain: **sharpened.**

- Time to recover: **verified.**

The Phantom may rise again.

Or something worse.

But now, the organization doesn't face it alone.

Not with a council.

Not with a doctrine.

With muscle memory.

Badge Earned: *"The Orchestrator"*

Wisdom Gained: *"Resilience is not built in quiet rooms. It is forged in fire."*

What do you do next?

[26] Explain Calmly and Hold Your Ground

Without documentation, it'll happen again.

[53] The Final Walls

The council spoke. Now you build.

[64] The Next Blade

The mission outlives you. That's how you win.

[66] A New Battlefield

You gave them the tools. But that doesn't mean they'll use them.

Chapter 53

The Final Walls

The drill proved it: your defenses hold under fire.

The council stands ready.

But you know the truth —

a castle with unfinished walls invites siege.

The high-risk zones are fortified. The crown jewels secured.

But shadows still linger:

- Legacy support systems, long overlooked

- Low-tier business apps with access they never needed

- Development sandboxes — once safe, now potential corridors for attackers

Your mission is clear: *complete the fortress.*

You map the remaining zones:

- Internal tools that never should have had direct lines to sensitive systems

- Old servers running legacy code — segment, monitor, plan for retirement

- Contractor portals — default deny, identity enforce, monitor tight

The deployment begins:

- **Microsegments drop into place** — no trust without proof

- **ACLs tuned with precision** — no broad rules, no "temporary" exceptions

- **Telemetry activated** — what was once invisible now glows beneath the spotlight

Your SOC watches:

- **Lateral movement attempts** — blocked

- **Unauthorized calls** — denied

- **New baselines** — set, clean, strong

No more hidden paths. No more easy prey. Your network now reflects your vision: ***segmented, hardened, resilient.***

And with it, you feel it — not the end of a fight, but the beginning of command. **The network lives now. And it lives by your design.**

Badge Earned: *"The Fortress Maker"*

Wisdom Gained: *"Every connection permitted without purpose is a future regret."*

What do you do next?

[54] The Story Beyond the Walls

The walls held. But some stories live outside them.

[55] The Shield Beyond the Walls

You can't protect everything. But you can protect with others.

[56] The Vigil Never Ends

The breach didn't end things. It began your watch.

[57] The Unseen Blade

You didn't catch everything. Now it's time to find what remains.

Chapter 54

The Story Beyond the Walls

The fortress stands.

The network breathes — **segmented, fortified, vigilant.**

The people defend — *trained, aware, aligned.*

The council guides — *vigilant, unified, relentless.*

But resilience hoarded is resilience wasted.

The Phantom taught you.

The fire forged you.

Now, the story must travel.

You begin crafting the case study —

not for glory, but for guidance.

You map the journey:

- **The breach** — the Phantom's rise, the tunnels of deception, the cost in trust and time.

- **The response** — isolation, rebuild, the Ronin's hands on raw code, the night the network was reborn.

- **The strategy** — Zero Trust not as theory, but as action: segmentation, hardening, continuous validation.

- **The culture** — playbooks reforged, councils formed, people empowered.

You fill it with truth:

- **Metrics** — time to contain, recovery speeds, threat attempts blocked.

- **Lessons** — what failed, what worked, what changed forever.

- **Outcomes** — not just a safer network, but a stronger business, a more resilient organization.

You strip away the jargon. You write for CISOs, for boards, for engineers — for everyone who will face what you faced, and need a light forward.

The case study publishes.

The response is swift:

- "This is what we needed — real guidance, not platitudes."

- "We shared this with our board. It opened their eyes."

- "Thank you. We were lost on where to start. We aren't anymore."

Your fire forged defenses. ***Your story lights the way.***

Badge Earned: *"The Beacon"*

Wisdom Gained: *"Resilience shared is resilience multiplied."*

What do you do next?

[55] The Shield Beyond the Walls

Defense doesn't stop at your walls. It thrives in relationships.

[56] The Vigil Never Ends

Resilience is built day by day, alert by alert.

[57] The Unseen Blade

There's always something lurking in the quiet.

[58] The Network Yet to Come

You shaped what came before. Now help shape what's next.

The Shield Beyond the Walls

The fortress is strong.

The people are ready.

The council is vigilant.

Your story has begun to guide others.

But you know this: **no network is an island.**

The Phantom didn't breach alone. It slipped in through trusted links — partners, platforms, connections that looked safe... until they weren't.

If resilience is to last, it must extend beyond your walls.

You draft the initiative.

Not as policy alone. As partnership.

- **Shared security standards**: Baselines for all suppliers — identity controls, encryption requirements, patch cadences.

- **Third-party risk assessments**: Not annually. Not quarterly. Continuous. Adaptive. Driven by real threat signals.

- **Shared threat intelligence**: You'll warn your partners. They'll warn you. No more silos between allies.

- **Integration hardening**: Every API, every SFTP, every link — validated, logged, monitored.

- **Incident response alignment**: When one is attacked, all respond — together, faster, smarter.

You present it to leadership. To procurement. To legal. To partners.

"This isn't just about protecting us," you say.

"This is the Ronin way — not just defending the gate,

but standing guard for those beyond it.

It's about protecting everyone who depends on us

— and who we depend on."

The response:

- **"We're in. Let's define the roadmap."**

- **"We've needed this. We've seen the same gaps."**

- **"Let's make this an industry standard, not just our initiative."**

The Phantom came through the supply chain once. It will not do so again — not easily, not quietly, **not without meeting the shield you now build together.**

Badge Earned: *"The Shield Bearer"*

Wisdom Gained: *"Your resilience is only as strong as those you trust."*

What do you do next?

[56] The Vigil Never Ends

You've built the shield. Now stay alert beside it.

[57] The Unseen Blade

Not every ally stayed clean. Some ghosts still linger.

[58] The Network Yet to Come

The network's growing. Be ready for what's coming next.

[59] The First Stones of Tomorrow

Trust is built on more than tech. Shape the mindset.

Chapter 56

The Vigil Never Ends

The walls are built.

The network breathes with purpose.

The supply chain shield rises.

But the Ronin knows — no defense is eternal unless it evolves.

The council is strong, forged in fire, tested in drills.

But strength, unchallenged, dulls. Plans, unreviewed, decay. Metrics, unmeasured, lie.

You take up the next mission — not to build walls, but cadence. *A rhythm of resilience.*

You design the continuous improvement plan — not as a report, but as a living cycle.

- **Quarterly risk reviews**: The council will gather — not just to hear updates, but to challenge them. What changed? What's emerging? What's being missed?

- **Threat horizon scanning**: The cyber threat landscape won't wait for annual reports. You integrate real-time threat intel feeds, AI-driven trend analysis, industry collaboration.

- **Tabletop and live-fire exercises**: No more once-a-year drills. You schedule layered tests — from simulated phishing to supply chain breach scenarios, with random triggers.

- **Metrics that matter**: Not patch counts. Not box-checking. Time to detect. Time to contain. Time to recover. Time to learn.

- **Resilience retrospectives**: After every exercise, after every incident — what worked, what failed, what changes now?

You present the plan.

The council doesn't just nod — they commit.Not out of habit, but belief.

They see it. They carry it.

The work isn't finished.

It never will be.

And that's exactly the point.

Badge Earned: *"The Keeper of the Flame"*

Wisdom Gained: *"Resilience is not a project. It is a practice."*

What do you do next?

[57] The Unseen Blade

You know better than to assume it's truly over.

[61] The Coalition of the Willing

You don't stand alone. Not anymore.

[64] The Next Blade

Your watch will end—but the mission will go on.

[65] The Watcher Returns to the Shadows

No headlines. No noise. Just silence, vigilance, readiness.

Chapter 57

The Unseen Blade

Your fortress stands firm.

The council sharpens its vigilance.

The supply chain is shielded.

Continuous improvement pulses through every segment.

But the Ronin knows: **No defender sees all their own flaws.**

Your internal teams have done their part.

The Red Team has tested, prodded, breached—and been blocked.

Now, it's time for something more:

New eyes. New blades. The unknown made visible.

You draft the engagement:

- **Scope:** Nothing is off-limits. On-prem, cloud, vendor connections, forgotten corners.

- **Rules:** Simulate the real—phishing, physical intrusion, social engineering, rogue code, poisoned supply chain.

- **Objective:** Not just gaps. Response times. Blind spots. Human failure.

Truth, not just technicals.

You bring in a team known not just for breaking—but for teaching through the break.

They go quiet.

And then, without warning, it begins:

- **A phishing campaign aimed at HR** — blocked by modern identity controls.

- **A rogue device inserted into an open port** — flagged and shut down in seconds.

- **API abuse routed through a trusted partner** — sink-holed before data left the wire.

But also...

- **A forgotten debug account** — exploited briefly before containment.

- **A social engineering call** — convincing enough to earn one misplaced click.

No breach. But a lesson.

Always a lesson.

The team delivers its report:

"You're resilient. Not invulnerable. Here's what the next wave will test."

You nod.

Because the blade you don't see is the one that cuts deepest.

And today — **you saw more than before.**

Badge Earned: *"Seeker of Shadows"*

Wisdom Gained: *"The wise invite attack — before it finds them."*

What do you do next?

[58] The Network Yet to Come

You can't see it — but it's already changing.

[59] The First Stones of Tomorrow

Even broken ground can become a fortress.

[60] The Shield Tested Together

If you stand together, the next cut might miss.

[61] The Coalition of the Willing

The unseen blade returns. This time, you're ready.

Chapter 58

The Network Yet to Come

The fortress stands. The council is vigilant.

The outsiders have tested your walls and revealed fresh truths.

But the Ronin sees further.

Because one truth never fades:

- No architecture is safe forever.

- No defense is future-proof if built for the past.

The Phantom was a creature of yesterday's shadows.

Tomorrow's threats will be smarter. Faster. Quieter.

And so you begin: **The design of what comes next.**

You wipe the whiteboards clean. You set aside legacy.

You imagine resilience not bolted on — but **born in.**

Your principles sharpen into truths:

- **Identity is the perimeter** — every packet, every request tied to a verifiable identity: human, machine, or process.

- **Dynamic segmentation** — boundaries that shift in real time, shaped by risk and trust, not static IPs.

- **Zero standing privilege** — access that exists only when needed, for only as long as necessary.

- **Cloud-native. Hybrid-strong.** No brittle bridges — just seamless security across environments.

- **AI–assisted defense** — machine-speed detection and response, guided by human wisdom.

- **Built–in chaos** — resilience tested not by theory, but by simulated failure.

You sketch the future — not a diagram, but a **living blueprint**:

- Service meshes with embedded policy enforcement

- Policy–as–code defining every connection and exception

- Immutable infrastructure — trusted, reproducible, unalterable

- Integration with supply chain assurance, business continuity, and crisis muscle memory

Your team leans in. Not just compliant — **committed**.

Because this isn't just about security anymore.

It's vision. It's evolution. It's readiness.

The next Phantom won't catch you off guard.

Because the next network won't wait to be tested.

It will be born ready.

Badge Earned: *"The Visionary Architect"*

Wisdom Gained: *"The best defense is built for the threats you cannot yet see."*

What do you do next?

[59] The First Stones of Tomorrow

What you've learned becomes the foundation.

[60] The Shield Tested Together

The best network is one that stands together.

[61] The Coalition of the Willing

You see what's coming — and who'll be ready.

[64] The Next Blade

You wrote the first verse. Now let them sing the next.

Chapter 59

The First Stones of Tomorrow

A vision can inspire. A vision can unite.

But without action, it's just a dream.

The future network is bold.

Dynamic. Resilient by design, not by patch.

But vision alone means nothing — **now it must be built.**

You chart the pilot deployments — carefully, deliberately:

- **Low-risk zones first:** areas where you can experiment without risking critical operations.

- **Cloud-native workloads:** the perfect proving ground for identity-centric, policy - driven architectures.

- **Dev environments:** places where chaos engineering can test your assumptions without breaking business flow.

You assemble your pilot task force:

- Network architects

- Cloud engineers

- Identity specialists

- DevSecOps champions

- Business owners who see innovation as strength, not risk

The deployment begins:

- Policy-as-code templates replace manual configurations — rules that adapt, enforced at machine speed.

- Just–in–time access grants flow seamlessly, no more standing privilege, no more forgotten admin keys.

- AI–assisted telemetry monitors every connection, alerting on deviations in real time.

- Chaos engineering injects failure — and the system self–heals, or the gap is revealed and closed.

And with each pilot zone, confidence grows:

- Systems prove resilient under simulated attack

- Access requests follow strict, auditable paths

- The network learns, adapts, strengthens

Your team sees it too.

"This isn't just better security," one engineer says.

"It's a better way to work."

The first stones of the future fortress are laid.

Solid. Tested. Real.

Badge Earned: *"The Builder of Tomorrow"*

Wisdom Gained: *"A vision means nothing until it is forged in action."*

What do you do next?

[60] The Shield Tested Together

It was never just about you. Together, you stood tall.

[61] The Coalition of the Willing

It's their turn — but you'll be watching.

[64] The Next Blade

Your name may fade, but your actions will echo.

[65] The Watcher Returns to the Shadows

You disappear from the directory. But never from the mission.

Chapter 60

The Shield Tested Together

The pilots are live. The new architecture breathes.

Your core is hardened. Your people trained.

Your processes tight.

But as any Ronin knows:

A fortress can fall not from within, but from the forgotten door down the road.

You remember how the Phantom first entered.

Not through brute force. **But through trust.**

That mistake won't be made again.

Now you test the outer shield — not alone, but shoulder to shoulder with those who share your risk.

You call the partners.

- Third-party vendors with critical access

- Cloud service providers

- B2B integration points

- Logistics, legal, and customer-facing allies

You don't ask them for a drill.

You invite them into a shared defense exercise.

The scope is bold:

- Simulated breach of a partner's identity stack

- Compromised system attempting lateral movement into your shared data zone

- Cloud platform outage mid-transaction — can you recover, route, or notify fast enough?

- Misinformation campaign aimed at trust in the ecosystem

The scenario plays out in real time:

- Telemetry flows across organizations

- Alerts are shared, actions coordinated

- A compromised integration point is isolated — not blamed, but secured

- Confusion minimized — because the playbooks were aligned

- Customer trust maintained through synchronized comms

You watch the network behave not as isolated nodes — but as a **resilient alliance.**

People move faster than protocols. Trust and transparency become tactical assets.

At the close, the debrief feels different:

"This wasn't a drill. It was survival—practiced together."

"We should repeat this quarterly — even bring in our own vendors next time."

"We were fast because we were informed. That's the power of partnership."

The Phantom found cracks in your chain once.

Now, those cracks are filled with vigilance. **And sealed with trust.**

Badge Earned: *"The Alliance Forged"*

Wisdom Gained: *"Real resilience doesn't stop at the boundary — it links arms with others."*

What do you do next?

[61] The Coalition of the Willing

The fight's not over. But now you won't fight it alone.

[64] The Next Blade

They're ready. Because you were.

[65] The Watcher Returns to the Shadows

You step back. The shield stays up.

[66] A New Battlefield

The battlefield shifts. And you're still ready.

Chapter 61

The Coalition of the Willing

The drill was a success.

Not because every move was perfect — but because every flaw surfaced became a shared lesson, not a private shame.

And now, the Ronin's gaze shifts outward.

If resilience is the new battlefield, then isolation is the enemy.

You've seen the patterns:

- The same threats hit different sectors days apart.

- The same attacker infrastructure targets banks, then hospitals, then manufacturers.

- The same vulnerability is patched by one org... while another falls.

Enough.

You begin to draft the framework for something bigger — something bold.

- **Cross-industry collaboration** — not just "information sharing," but **action** coordination.

- **Shared threat intelligence exchanges** — near real-time feeds between sectors: finance, healthcare, energy, logistics, government.

- **Mutual playbook alignment** — map incident response and escalation pathways so that when one is hit, others don't wait.

- **Joint tabletop exercises** — simulate multi-sector crises, because no attack stays in one lane anymore.

- **A resilience guild** — not a formal body, but a coalition of the willing. Not compliance. Conviction.

You host the first summit.

No keynotes. No vendor pitches. Just peers in the fight.

CISOs, resilience leads, ops directors — **tired of going it alone.**

You open with the story of the Phantom.

Not dramatized. Not bragged.

Just the truth: **what was missed, what was rebuilt, what was shared.**

And then... silence.

Nods. Pens scribbling. Minds racing.

One CISO speaks up:

> **"We've fought alone long enough.**
>
> **Let's build the map we all needed five years ago."**

And just like that, it begins.

The Ronin's journey becomes a shared path.

The firewall that once failed becomes a spark for collective strength.

Badge Earned: *"The Coalition Architect"*

Wisdom Gained: *"A lone shield may stop a blade. But a wall of shields turns battle into momentum."*

What do you do next?

[64] The Next Blade

You helped build it. Now let others lead it.

[65] The Watcher Returns to the Shadows

No signature needed — your work speaks for itself.

[66] A New Battlefield

You'll fight again — just with different armor.

[68] The Firewall Sleeps, But the Blade Remains

Even in peace, the blade must remain sharpened.

Chapter 62

The Day the Network Stood Still

You've rebuilt the network.

You've trained your people.

You've linked shields with partners and even competitors.

You've tested the defenses. Hardened every layer.

But now comes the deeper question—one no architecture diagram can answer:

Can the business survive when everything stops?

Because cyber resilience isn't just blocking malware or hardening firewalls.

It's keeping the company breathing when chaos strikes.

And so you begin: **the business continuity test**.

This time, it's not about network tunnels or packet flow.

It's about **orders, customers, operations, reputations**.

The scenario is crafted in silence:

- An attack corrupts internal DNS and disrupts core system access.

- The CRM and ERP platforms are simultaneously declared compromised.

- Communications falter — Slack goes dark, email delayed, phones rerouted.

- A regulatory inquiry is triggered mid-incident — timing

engineered for maximum stress.

The exercise begins. No warning. No cheat codes.

The executive floor is asked to reroute operations manually.

The fulfillment team is handed paper backup logs.

Finance attempts to process payroll without primary systems.

IT, security, legal, and comms huddle under pressure, not knowing what's real or simulated.

And still, the business moves.

Not fast. Not flawlessly. But forward.

- Continuity runbooks kick in.

- Shadow communications channels rise.

- Decisions are made with imperfect information — and held.

When it ends, there's no applause. Just deep exhales.

Then — the real work: the debrief.

Every misstep noted.

Every confusion addressed.

Every small victory amplified.

And in the room, something new:

confidence not in the systems, but in the people.

In the organization's ability to adapt. To endure. To lead.

The Phantom tried to break you with disruption.

Now you've turned disruption into a muscle memory.

Badge Earned: *"The Continuity Commander"*

Wisdom Gained: *"Real resilience isn't staying online. It's staying operational when nothing else works."*

What do you do next?

[64] The Next Blade

Others will rise. Make sure they're ready.

[65] The Watcher Returns to the Shadows

You've earned the silence. Use it well.

[66] A New Battlefield

Stillness is only a pause. The fight returns.

[68] The Firewall Sleeps, But the Blade Remains

The firewall may rest — but the blade remains.

Chapter 63

The Ronin Doctrine

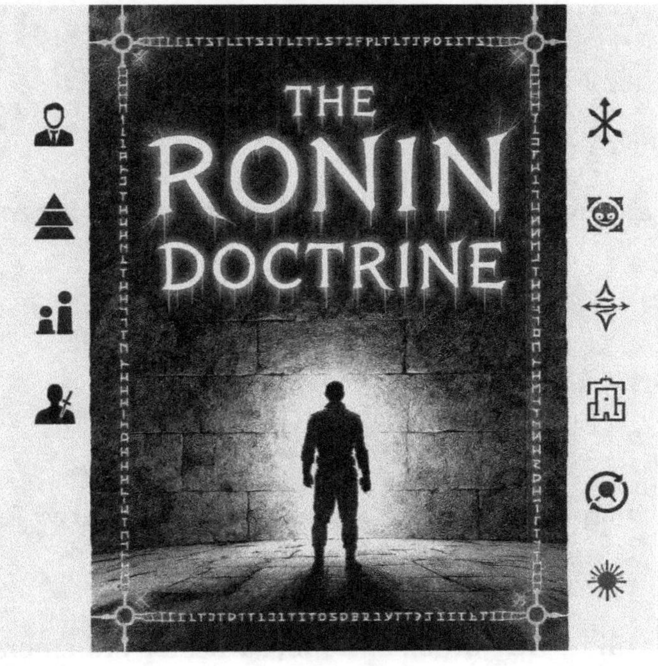

Battles were fought. Walls rebuilt.

Allies forged. Ghosts hunted. Shadows revealed.

And now, the Ronin knows it's time — not to end the journey, but to leave a map for those who will follow.

You open a clean document.

Not a policy. Not a playbook.

A doctrine. A philosophy.

A blade etched in memory—held high for those yet to face the dark.

At the top, you write:

The Ronin Doctrine:

Principles of Cyber Resilience in a Fractured Age

You don't fill it with jargon or padded mission statements.

You carve in truth, earned line by line, breach by breach, choice by choice.

The Ronin Doctrine (Core Tenets)

1. Know Your Infrastructure — And Your Blind Spots

Every unseen service, every unchecked tunnel, every silent dependency is a battlefield waiting to be chosen by your enemy. Map them. Own them.

2. Identity Is the New Perimeter

If you can't verify it, you can't trust it. And if you can't revoke it instantly, it doesn't belong.

3. Segmentation Is Survival

When—not if—something breaks, your architecture must fail inward, not outward. Divide with purpose. Connect with proof.

4. Detection Is Not Enough — Response Must Be Reflex

If you have to decide whether to act, you've already lost time. Automate what can be automated. Train what must be human.

5. Build for Failure — Then Simulate It

Chaos is not the enemy. Chaos is the instructor. Test yourself until failure becomes familiar, and recovery becomes routine.

6. Culture Eats Policy for Breach–fast

If your people don't believe in the mission, no badge scanner or MFA prompt will save you. Train, empower, trust.

7. Resilience Must Extend Beyond Your Walls

No vendor is "third–party" in a breach. Share intelligence. Test together. Survive together.

8. Your Story Matters

Document everything. Share the wins. Own the failures. Your transparency may save someone else's network tomorrow.

You don't just publish it.

You **read it aloud** to the council, to the SOC, to the new hires who never lived through the Phantom.

You see the impact — eyes narrow, heads nod.

These are not rules.

They are rallying cries.

The Doctrine is not final —

it will evolve, as all defenders must.

But now, your legacy has shape.

It has weight. It has a name.

Badge Earned: *"The Philosopher Defender"*

Wisdom Gained: *"Resilience isn't a technology stack. It's a way of thinking — and a way of leading."*

What do you do next?

[64] The Next Blade

You were never meant to be the only one.

[65] The Watcher Returns to the Shadows

The Ronin moves on, but the path remains.

[66] A New Battlefield

You don't stay still. Not now. Not ever.

[68] The Firewall Sleeps, But the Blade Remains

This isn't the end. Just the pause between strikes.

Chapter 64

The Next Blade

The Doctrine is written.

The fortress holds.

The shadows have cleared.

But the Ronin knows — no firewall, no strategy, no vision endures... unless someone carries it forward.

The war against chaos is not won once. It is won daily — through vigilance, curiosity, and conviction.

And so you begin your most important mission yet:

mentoring the one who comes next.

You don't post a job opening.

You watch — for someone who asks the right questions when others look away.

Someone who doesn't just want to block attacks, but to understand them.

Someone who sees security not as control, but as stewardship.

You find them.

- **Young**, but not naïve.

- **Smart**, but not reckless.

- **Curious. Confident. Quietly dangerous** — in the right way.

You bring them in.

Not with ceremony, but with responsibility.

You show them:

- How the Phantom moved — not just technically, but psy–chologically.

- Why segmentation worked — and when it almost didn't.

- What it means to hold the line not for policy, but for people.

- How leadership listens first, acts second, and documents third.

You don't teach them to become you.

You teach them to become better.

One day, you hand them the console key — not with a speech, but with silence.

You nod. They nod back.

No oath. No ceremony. **Just trust.**

The fortress is still theirs to defend.

The network is still a battlefield.

But now, the line is held by another blade.

The Ronin steps back — not to vanish,

but to sharpen a new edge in the shadows.

Badge Earned: *"The Torchbearer"*

Wisdom Gained: *"The true legacy of a warrior is not the fight they won — but the warrior they shaped to keep fighting."*

What do you do next?

[61] The Coalition of the Willing

The mission outlives the warrior. Share what you've learned.

[65] The Watcher Returns to the Shadows

Sometimes the most powerful stance is silence.

[66] A New Battlefield

Even as you pass the sword, keep your armor ready.

[68] The Firewall Sleeps, But the Blade Remains

The blade rests. But never dulls.

Chapter 65

The Watcher Returns to the Shadows

The student now holds the console.

The Doctrine echoes in the halls of leadership.

The supply chain is shielded.

The council remains vigilant.

And yet... **the Ronin does not rest.**

Because you know the truth behind all systems:

Peace is only the silence between storms.

The Phantom may have been broken, but the pattern remains.

New threats will rise — not as echoes of the old, but as evolutions.

Faster. Subtler. More convincing. More personal.

You broke the Phantom's pattern once.

But patterns always try to reform.

You don't raise a glass. You raise your guard.

No parade. No headline. Just a quiet exit — and a quiet return to the edge.

Not from the company — **but from the spotlight.**

You return to the dark places:

- Old audit trails.

- Forgotten API keys.

- Low–traffic ports where yesterday's devs left today's vulnerability.

- Dependency chains with unknown authors.

- Machine learning pipelines mutating without oversight.

You walk the edges of the network like a blade through tall grass — silent, sharp, deliberate.

You scan code not because it's urgent — but because it's time.

You chase whispers in logs not yet known to be malicious.

You test detection tools by evading them — reminding them, and yourself, that complacency is the most dangerous exploit of all.

Sometimes, you pause.

You reread the Doctrine. Not to remember — but to **reflect**.

"Resilience is not a project. It is a practice."

"The best defense is built for the threats you cannot yet see."

"The true legacy of a warrior is not the fight they won —

but the warrior they shaped to keep fighting."

You smile. Just slightly. Then the silence reminds you why you stay.

The network is quiet tonight.

But the Ronin is awake.

Badge Earned: *"The Eternal Sentinel"*

Wisdom Gained: *"The mission never ends. Only the enemies change."*

THE END...?

Or perhaps just a checkpoint.

- Play again — and choose the reckless path

- Start over as the new Ronin

- Follow the Phantom... and see where its trail leads next

*As you fade back into the perimeter, one last encrypted message appears...***UNLISTED NODE — KATANA-5**

- Go to **Chapter 69**

Chapter 66

A New Battlefield

The SOC dims. Dashboards quiet. Alerts rest — but never vanish.

Your Doctrine lives. Your successor thrives.

Your name? Nearly forgotten. **And that's the point.**

But the Ronin's path is never meant to settle. It bends, breaks, reforms — wherever the next threat emerges.

And today, it arrives.

An encrypted message hits your private inbox — a vector no longer monitored, retired long ago.

It contains only coordinates, a time, and a company name that surfaced in breach reports but never in public statements.

You've seen this pattern before — high-impact targets moving faster than their defenses. A tech startup scaling too fast. A medical device firm pushing firmware updates over open channels. An aerospace vendor blending simulation and reality without authentication logic.

Not the same Phantom — but something like it. New mask. Same hunger. The network hums, alive with the same reckless energy you've hunted before. **And silence — you've learned — is never safe.**

You pack light.

No celebration. No parade. Just a quiet nod to the shadows that trained you.

Before you go, you leave behind a note on your desk:

"Not the end. Just another perimeter."

You walk into a different lobby.

Different badge. Different architecture. Different culture.

Same mission. Same fire. Same blade.

You shake hands with the CEO.

They smile, unaware of the storm they narrowly avoided — or may already be in.

You speak your first words:

"Let's talk about where your risk really lives."

Outside, the city hums. And somewhere deep within — **the Phantom listens.**

And just like that, the Ronin rises again.

Badge Earned: *"The Wanderer"*

Wisdom Gained: *"A true defender is never done — only deployed elsewhere."*

Before you step into the new war, a legacy system whispers one final note...

- Go to **Chapter 69**

Chapter 67

Echoes in the Mesh

Far from the hardened network you rebuilt, beyond the resilience council, past the partners and the Doctrine...

A different network hums. It's not segmented. It's not monitored.

Its logs are incomplete.

Its firewall still trusts what it shouldn't.

And through it — something moves.

> ***Something fast. Something quiet. Something new.***

Not the Phantom. **Worse.**

Where the Phantom cloaked itself in deception, this one hides in **visibility**.

> ***It doesn't evade detection —***
>
> ***it lives within it.***
>
> ***It mimics trusted behavior.***
>
> ***It speaks with your agents.***
>
> ***It flows through your telemetry.***
>
> ***It watches. It waits.***
>
> ***It learns.***

It has a name — not one given by defenders, but by itself:

The Meshwalker.

The new company, the new architecture, the new ally you trained — they're all in its line of sight.

And you don't even know it yet.

It doesn't want access.

It wants influence.

It wants to shape your response before you even know you're compromised.

And somewhere, deep in the mesh... it's already listening.

But it doesn't know one thing:

The Ronin has returned.

You've faced deception. You've fought inside the firewalls. You've hunted ghosts.

Now you'll fight the adversary hiding in plain sight.

"Not a battle of fire. A war of perception."

Threat Unlocked: *"The Meshwalker"*

New Mission Cue: *"Cyber Ronin: Volume II — The Shadow Mesh"*

The Mesh shifts. A hidden node activates. It's meant for you.

- Go to **Chapter 69**

Chapter 68

The Firewall Sleeps, But the Blade Remains

The data centers cool.

The dashboards idle.

The alerts settle into patterns — calm, for now.

Somewhere in the architecture, a security sensor flickers once, then stabilizes.

A false positive. Or maybe not.

The rebuilt firewall — once twisted by the Phantom's deception — now hums with precision.

Segmented. Hardened. Watched.

Not perfect. But practiced.

And above it all, invisible to the untrained eye, is the mark of the Ronin:

- A configuration template with no name.

- A detection rule written in a style only one person uses.

- A comment buried deep in the logs:

"If you're reading this,

you've already waited too long to respond."

The new defender holds the line now.

They train. They lead. They question.

Exactly as you did.

But in quiet hours, when the network is still,

They sometimes notice something unusual:

- A stray packet rerouted faster than the system should allow.

- A rule that appears seconds before they write it.

- A log entry signed only with a katana emoji.

The Ronin is gone.

But not absent.

You walk a new perimeter now.

Unseen. Unnamed. Unafraid.

Watching new technologies rise, and with them, new dangers.

AI agents conversing without supervision.

Shadow clouds spun up in seconds.

Not networks, but clusters of intent. Identity. Influence.

And in that space... a shape is forming.

It isn't loud. It doesn't strike. It shifts.

It guides. It suggests.

The Meshwalker.

You sense its presence — not as code, but as influence.

A nudge here. A delayed alert there.

Subtle. Patient. Whispering its way through systems people think are secure.

But you are not people.

You are the Ronin.

And you don't wait for threats.

You become the one they fear is watching.

The firewall sleeps.

But the blade remains — sharp, unseen, and ready.

END OF BOOK 1

Cyber Ronin: The Phantom Firewall

Badge Earned: *"The Last Wall"*

Wisdom Gained: *"True resilience isn't a reaction. It's a readiness without need for permission."*

The firewall rests. But something stirs beneath the surface — one last message.

- Go to **Chapter 69**

Chapter 69

The Final Log

[SECURE ENTRY — UNLISTED NODE]

Encryption Level: KATANA-5

Voice Signature: Confirmed

Subject: Final reflections, unknown observer

If you're reading this, then one of three things has happened:

- You've inherited a network that looks clean — but isn't.

- You're tracking something you can't name yet — but feel.

- Or worse: you're dealing with something that thinks you're the threat.

Whichever it is... welcome. You've stepped onto the path.

It doesn't end — it deepens. The Phantom was only the first.

It wasn't smart — just clever. Opportunistic. Fast.

But it taught me everything I needed to remember:

- That trust is always the first exploit.

- That every system is only as resilient as the last person who touched it.

- That the worst attacks don't just target systems — they shape behavior.

I left behind the tools. I wrote the Doctrine. I trained the next.

But there will always be gaps. Gaps no tool can fill.

That's why you're here.

Not to be perfect. But to be present.

To notice what no one else does. To act when others hesitate.

To question even the things that look like safety.

If you're lucky, your war will be quiet.

But if it isn't — know this:

You are not alone. You never were.

There are more of us than they think. Some in boardrooms.

Some in basements. Some hidden in plain code. All watching.

We don't wear capes.

We don't beg for compliance budgets.

We carry blades made of insight, silence, and resolve.

You are a Cyber Ronin now.

Welcome to the edge. **End of Log.**

File archived to unindexed memory sector: **SHADOW_MESH/SEED_01**

Badge Earned: *"The Edgewalker"*

Wisdom Gained: *"Not all firewalls burn. Some simply wait."*

Behind the Firewall

A Word from the Creator

This book began with a question: **What if a cybersecurity training tool didn't feel like a training tool at all?**

I've spent years in the trenches of cybersecurity—navigating chaos, negotiating with risk, and occasionally wondering why the blinking light turned red *again*. Over time, I realized something: while policies and frameworks are critical, **real learning comes from experience—especially the kind that sticks with you.**

So I built this book to simulate those moments. The urgent decisions. The conflicting priorities. The doubt. And yes, the occasional voice in your head whispering, *"Don't click that..."*

Cyber Ronin: The Phantom Firewall is part adventure, part reflection, and part therapy for anyone who's ever tried to secure an organization while the world burned around them. It's a story—and a challenge: to think differently, act intentionally, and laugh at the absurdity of it all.

If you found yourself shouting at the page, pausing to think, or laughing at how close it hit to home—**mission accomplished**. Thank you for stepping into the Ronin's boots. Now... go patch something. *Or at least pretend you did.*

If this book helped, inspired, or made you laugh at the pain—drop me a note. *We're all in this weird fight together.* — S.B.

Decision Paths

Which Cyber Ronin Are You?

There's more than one way to breach—or defend—a system.

In Cyber Ronin: The Phantom Firewall, your journey is shaped by the choices you make. But this isn't just about right or wrong—it's about strategy, instincts, and trade-offs.

Below are the core Decision Archetypes woven throughout the story:

The Warrior Path — *Action Over Analysis*

You strike fast, act boldly, and aren't afraid to make some noise. You may win by force... or go down in a blaze of digital glory.

- **Traits:** Aggressive, decisive, risk-tolerant

- **Outcomes:** Can trigger quick wins—or critical missteps

The Analyst Path — *Think, Then Strike*

You pause. You probe. You play the long game. Victory is in the details, and timing is everything.

- **Traits:** Strategic, cautious, data-driven

- **Outcomes:** Reveals hidden truths—unless you wait too long

The Deceiver Path — *Nothing Is What It Seems*

You bend rules, wear masks, and mislead attackers (and maybe allies). In a world built on trust, deception is its own weapon.

- **Traits:** Clever, adaptive, manipulative

- **Outcomes:** High payoff, high risk—and not always ethical

The Leadership Path — *Guide the Many, Not Just Yourself*

You step up when others falter. You make tough calls. Your focus is the mission—even when it costs you personally.

- **Traits:** Accountable, visionary, resilient

- **Outcomes:** Builds loyalty and long-term resilience—or collapses under pressure

The Chaos Path — *YOLOsec*

You ignore protocol. You follow gut instinct. Sometimes it works. Sometimes it's a disaster. Either way—it's never boring.

- **Traits:** Unpredictable, instinctive, rebellious

- **Outcomes:** Can uncover brilliance—or total digital chaos

And Yes... *You Can Loop Back*

Certain decisions may reveal alternate timelines, secret backdoors, or restart points. You might think you're done... until the story isn't done with you.

No one plays just one path forever. Your journey shifts with every breach, every badge, every choice.

The Packet

(Day 0 Materials — Redacted)

The orientation wasn't much — three folders tossed onto your desk. You opened them all. This is what you found inside.

==================================

Folder 1: Transition

==================================

Welcome Letter — Security Orientation

- During your first days here, you'll notice security woven into nearly every workflow. This isn't about paranoia — it's about preserving the trust our teams have built.

- Our network faces a constant hum of noise and probes. Most are harmless scans. Some are not. Your vigilance is part of our defense.

- Never push unverified code or data into production. Even "safe" commits can introduce rot if the source isn't trusted.

- Onboarding will provide you with the credentials, tokens, and policies you need. Keep them close, and keep them secure.

- Training is ongoing. The threat landscape doesn't pause, and neither should your learning.

- Tests of our incident response are scheduled and unscheduled. Treat both with the seriousness they deserve.

- Record your actions during any suspected incident. Memory is flawed; logs are evidence.

- Understand that security is shared — no role is exempt, and no system is too small to protect.

- Signs of compromise are often subtle: a single log line, a mismatch in a checksum, a server behaving slightly out of rhythm.

- Take those signals seriously. Escalate early. Let the SOC decide if it's noise or a breach.

- Manipulated data is worse than missing data. Always verify integrity before you rely on a file, a feed, or a fact.

- In the event of conflicting information, default to the most verified source, not the most convenient one.

- Review the escalation paths in your wallet card. Know the people behind those numbers.

- Reports must be accurate, even if incomplete. Never embellish to fill gaps.

- Observing quietly can be as powerful as acting — but don't let quiet turn into inaction.

- Remember: mirrors can distort. What you see may not be the truth.

- Stay alert, trust the process, and you'll keep both yourself and the mission safe.

Orientation Checklist

- **Trust store:** install corporate root CA and VPN certificates.

- **Harden your laptop:** full-disk encryption on, screen lock ≤5 min, OS auto-updates enabled.

- **Register your security key:** add a FIDO2 hardware key and safely store backup codes.

- **Enroll in SSO:** confirm Okta profile, device posture checks, and least-privilege role are applied.

- **Enable endpoint protection:** verify EDR/AV is active and reporting healthy.

- **Familiarize with incident comms:** join the incident-response chat channel and (if applicable) the on-call app.

- **Initiate password manager:** set up the org vault; migrate any work creds to it.

- **Verify device management:** MDM enrolled, compliance green, VPN client configured.

- **Establish secure email settings:** Safe Links/Attachments on; report-phish add-in visible.

- **Set up secrets access:** request scoped access to the secrets vault; rotate any seeded API keys.

- **Enable backups/versioning:** in the approved cloud drive; perform a quick restore test of a sample file.

- **Validate access scope:** ticketing, repos, data shares; remove anything you don't need.

- **Educate yourself:** read the GAVEL card and skim the build-provenance/SBOM one-pager in this packet.

- **Note critical contacts:** SOC hotline, duty manager, and incident response lead.

Incident Response Wallet Card

Front:

Back:

ESCALATION STEPS

1. Contain safely
2. Preserve evidence
3. Notify SOC
4. Record ticket ID
5. Debrief within 24 hours

0x357CQDE

==

Folder 2: Legacy Risks

==

Facilities Work Order — Sub-Basement B

Location: Row 3, **DC-LEGACY01** "Heritage DC" Scope: Replace 3 rack fans, add 5 foam baffles, test 7-minute thermal run.

Note: "Label DO NOT TOUCH must remain. Unit participates in auth fallback."

Unsigned Log Extract

2025-02-08T02:11:59Z dc-legacy01[krb5]: ntlm_fallback disabled [sha=0f31a]

2025-02-08T02:14:11Z authd[2173]: okta_mfa push accepted [sha=4f2a1]

2025-02-08T02:15:02Z buildd[8891]: signer online: keyid=keystone-01 [sha=19c0e]

2025-02-08T02:17:44Z pkgctl[4420]: sbom delta created for release 1.14.3 [sha=7be51]

-----BEGIN CIRCULAR----- recorder: witness incomplete; hold mirrors until verified

2025-02-08T02:18:09Z backup[1140]: snapshot started [sha=2ad77]

2025-02-08T02:20:55Z router[7303]: aspath updated as-royal-7 via rpki ok [sha=c9d31]

Release Note / SBOM Excerpt

- agent-driver-legacy — sha256: ...f5d0

- dc-interop-bridge — sha256: ...f5d8

- libcrypto-2.4.1 — sha256: ...1a2e

- waf-ruleset — sha256: ...9c73

- sbom-indexer — sha256: ...0b11

===================================

Folder 3: Do Not Touch

===================================

Network Diagram

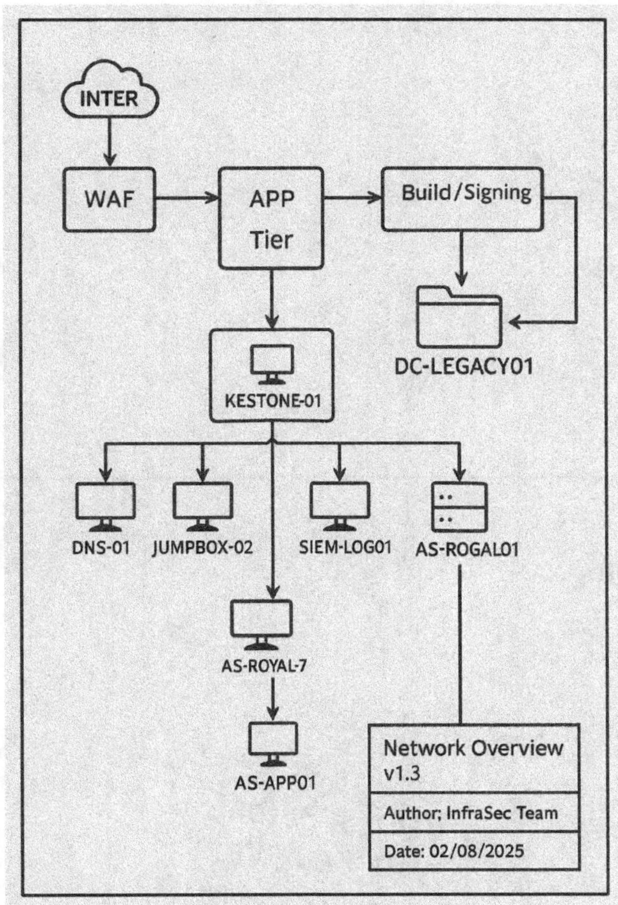

INI Config Dump

[auth]

host=dc–legacy01

realm=CORP.LOCAL

endpoint=/krb5/bridge

[doors]

open=3

close=3

[steps]

sequence=5

retry=5

[witnesses]

required=7

quorum=2/3

Sticky Note

VERiFY BEFORE YOU BELiEVE.
Re: DC-LEGACY01 — leave it alone until provenance check. — W